We hope you enjoy this
Please return or renew it ~~~~~~~~ date
You can renew ~~~~~~~~ **Jefferson** ~~~~~~~~ s
or by ~~~

Jefferson

JEAN-CLAUDE MOURLEVAT

TRANSLATED BY ROS SCHWARTZ
ILLUSTRATED BY ANTOINE RONZON

ANDERSEN PRESS
LONDON

For my children, who opened my eyes
JCM

First published in English in 2020 by
Andersen Press Limited
20 Vauxhall Bridge Road
London SW1V 2SA
www.andersenpress.co.uk

2 4 6 8 10 9 7 5 3 1

Originally published in French as Jefferson in 2018
by Gallimard Jeunesse

British Library Cataloguing in Publication Data available.

ISBN 978 1 78344 969 9

Printed and bound in Great Britain by Clays Ltd, Elcograf S.p.A.

Supported using public funding by
ARTS COUNCIL
ENGLAND

This book has been selected to receive financial assistance from English PEN's "PEN Translates!"
programme, supported by Arts Council England. English PEN exists to promote literature and our
understanding of it, to uphold writers' freedoms around the world, to campaign against the persecution
and imprisonment of writers for stating their views, and to promote the friendly co-operation of writers
and the free exchange of ideas. www.englishpen.org

Author's note

The land where this story begins is inhabited by animals who can walk on their hind legs, talk, borrow books from the library, fall in love, send text messages and go to the hairdresser's. The neighbouring country is home to humans, who are the most intelligent of animals.

1

The young hedgehog Jefferson Ponsonby-Smythe hummed to himself as he finished tidying his abode, *pom-pom-tiddly-pom*, like someone who was in a very good mood. When everything was hunky-dory, the brush shaken out of the window and the dustpan back on its nail, he set his oven timer so that his creamy potatoes would be cooked to perfection by the time he came home. Then he put on his jacket and fastened the middle button, noticing how the fabric puckered over his budding paunch. He'd have to cut down on the biscuits from now on.

He spritzed himself with *Fern* eau de toilette, went into the hallway and put on his spotlessly shiny shoes, placing first his right foot and then his left on the little stool. Then he slipped on his rucksack and went out. The reason he was so cheerful that morning was simple: he'd decided to go to the hairdresser's. It had suddenly struck him when he was getting washed and dressed that his elegant quiff was a mess. And one thing he hated was looking unkempt. Right! He'd go into town and have his quiff trimmed!

While there, he'd return the book he'd borrowed from the library the previous week, an adventure story called *Alone on the River*. The action took place on the Orinoco and the hero, a young human called Chuck, overcame a whole series of challenges with fearless courage. Solitude, hunger, thirst, mosquitoes, hostile forest-dwellers, torrential rain, scorching heat and wild animals ... Chuck triumphed over all adversity.

Snuggled under his blanket, his steaming cup of herbal tea on the bedside table, Jefferson had imagined that *he* was Chuck. He sometimes caught himself clenching his fists as he read, his eyes popping. In any case, the book had kept him awake till dawn two nights in a row. He'd especially loved the chapter where Chuck, lost in the jungle, tries to find his way using the star technique. You set off in one direction at random, walk straight ahead for fifty paces and then, if you find nothing, you go back to your starting point and try your luck in a different direction. He'd also enjoyed the chilling episode where Chuck, starving, decides to kill his dog and eat him to survive, but at the last minute he relents, starts to cry and spares the poor creature. On reading those pages, Jefferson had to rummage under his pillow for his handkerchief and dab his eyes. Later on in the story, the dog saves Chuck's life, paying him back in kind. Again, that brought tears to Jefferson's eyes. That's one of the best things about living alone: you can sing loudly and out of tune, wander around naked, eat whenever you like and cry unashamedly.

It was a glorious autumn morning. Jefferson locked his front door, put the key in his left trouser pocket, took his phone out of the other and texted the following message:

Dear Gilbert, don't come over this morning. I'm in town. I'm going to have my quiff trimmed at Cut 'n' Dye. I'll be back around lunchtime. I've put a potato dish in the oven, if you fancy it . . . Ciao, buddy!

Then off he set with a song in his heart. What more could he ask of life? He was blessed with robust health, he had a roof over his head, plenty of food, a wonderful friend in Gilbert the pig, and he lived

3

in the most delightful surroundings on the fringes of a beechwood.

The town was close by. You just had to walk downhill for a few minutes along a path lined with currant bushes and you soon came to the road. Jefferson followed this road, rounding bend after bend.

Was it because his thoughts were still with Chuck on the banks of the Orinoco? Or because he was already picturing himself in the gentle hands of Sophie, the young hairdresser's assistant who would shampoo him? Whatever the reason, it meant he crossed the road at an awkward spot, just after a tight bend.

A car heading away from the town came hurtling towards him at over eighty miles an hour. Jefferson caught only a glimpse of the two people inside. The driver was a tall, very thin human with a shaved head. He looked as if he'd had to fold himself up to fit his lanky frame into the car. The passenger, another human, much beefier, was wearing a woollen beanie and his elbow was resting on the door with the window wound down. The driver slammed on the brakes with a screech of tyres. Jefferson let out a terrible squeal, leaped out of the way and tumbled backwards into the ditch. The jeep swerved and the passenger barked out of the open window something that began with 'You . . .' and ended with '. . . hedgehog', preceded by an adjective that can't be repeated here.

'Same to you!' grunted Jefferson.

He watched the vehicle accelerate and vanish. He got to his feet, adjusted his clothes, felt his soaked bottom and wondered whether he should go home and get changed. He dithered for a moment and then decided he couldn't be bothered to walk all the way back. My trousers will dry out on the way, he said to himself. And he'd go to the library first. Then the wet patch would be gone by the time he saw Sophie, so she wouldn't think . . . goodness knows what.

Busy with these thoughts, he was aware that his heart was still thumping annoyingly. The incident had shaken him badly. He'd come within a whisker of death and it had nearly been 'Bye, bye, hedgehog!' That was life: one minute you feel light, joyful and carefree and then, in a split-second, everything changes. Happiness is so fragile, he said to himself, and tried to think about other things.

By the time he reached town, he was almost back to his usual chirpy self. He whistled as he sauntered up the high street and then took the left fork at the fountain. The staff at the public library knew him well and they greeted him with a delighted, 'Hello, Jefferson!'

'Did you enjoy it?' asked the librarian, a kindly mother duck with heart-shaped spectacles, as he handed *Alone on the River* in at the returns desk. He remembered that she was the one who'd suggested the book.

'Enjoy it? No!' he began, and then, because she looked crestfallen and he didn't want to tease her any longer, he added, 'I didn't *enjoy* it, I LOVED it. Thank you so much for your advice. I'm going to recommend it to my friend Gilbert.'

'Oh, Mr Jefferson,' said the librarian, blushing. 'You had me worried. And surprised, too, because I was certain that you'd find Chuck's adventures thrilling. You can renew it now if you like, and lend it to your friend yourself.'

He thanked her, then rooted around among the stacks for a while before perching casually on a corner of the radiator to flick through some magazines. Half an hour later, he left the library, *Alone on the River* still in his rucksack and his bottom almost dry.

*

The hair salon Cut 'n' Dye was at the very end of the same street. It was an unpretentious, old-fashioned shop which could only hold three customers at one time. Edgar, the owner, was a kindly, easy-going badger who had, in Jefferson's eyes, or rather ears, a rare and precious quality in a hairdresser: he was able to cut your hair in silence.

A customer of the salon for many years, Jefferson knew he wouldn't be deluged with chitchat. He smoothed his jacket, thrust out his chest, took a few deep breaths and cleared his throat. Supposing he invited Sophie for a drink when she finished work? A very good idea, that. An excellent idea, even. He would wait until Mr Edgar was on the telephone, for instance, and pluck up his courage: 'I say, Sophie, what time do you finish? Because I was thinking, um . . . I mean, I was saying to myself, as it were . . . that maybe . . .'

Sophie was Mr Edgar's niece, and had been taken on by her uncle, who was getting older, to help him out. Jefferson loved it when she shampooed him, massaging his head with her supple fingers. He adored it when she asked whether the water was too hot or too cold. Whatever the temperature, he would reply that it was perfect. She could have poured freezing or boiling water over him and he wouldn't have complained. Comfortably settled on the booster seat that was necessary given his diminutive height, he'd close his eyes with pleasure and imagine that she was his girlfriend. Because, although living alone has some benefits, as we've seen, sometimes it can feel . . . a little lonesome.

When Jefferson tried the handle, he was surprised to find that the door wouldn't open, even though the Cut 'n' Dye sign above it was illuminated and the metal shutter raised. He peered in to try and see through the curtains. The lights were on. A matronly nanny goat was asleep beneath a hood dryer, a plastic cap on her head. Everything seemed to be in order, except that there was no sign of the hairdresser, Mr Edgar, or of Sophie. Jefferson tapped on the window and waited. He tapped again, a little harder, to no avail, and, recalling that there was a window at the back, he decided to walk around the building.

The double window was open, but climbing in would be illegal, and there was nothing Jefferson hated more than breaking the law. He had always tried to keep to the rules, partly out of public-spiritedness but most of all, it has to be said, so that he'd be left in peace. So he went back to the front door, rapped on the glass again and, since nothing moved inside, came to the conclusion that he'd just have to go home.

Remorse stopped him in his tracks. What if something had happened . . . ? What if Sophie was in danger! The idea that he could be some sort of hero in the young badger's eyes prompted him to make a sudden and irresistible U-turn. Two minutes later, he was standing once more beneath the open window at the back of the building.

'Mr Edgar! Miss Sophie!' he called, and since no one bothered to reply, he mustered all his courage and heaved himself up through the window, at the risk of snagging his jacket.

He found himself in an office cluttered with bottles, boxes, mousses, shampoos and other hair products. The only sound he could hear from the front of the shop was that of the local radio. A gabbling voice was urging listeners to dial a premium number without delay, thanks to which, with a lot of luck, they'd win nothing at all. He advanced gingerly, and called out again: 'Mr Edgar? Miss Sophie? It's me, Jefferson. I took the liberty . . .'

The nanny goat was fast asleep under her hood, her half-open mouth revealing a perfect set of dentures, a thin trickle of saliva dribbling slowly down her chin. She appeared to be floating in a gentle state of rapture. Perhaps she was dreaming of her great-grandkids.

Jefferson walked around the first customer chair, which was unoccupied, and instantly spotted Mr Edgar's cream-coloured shoes pointing upwards. They were unmistakeable: a pair of hairdresser's shoes which the good man was always boasting about, saying they were as comfortable as bedroom slippers. Another step and Jefferson could see his legs lying parallel on the floor, then his white coat carefully buttoned all the way down, and then, further up his body, the big scissors, one blade plunged up to the hilt in Mr Edgar's chest.

The bloodstain spreading from the wound reminded Jefferson of a map of Madagascar. Ironically, the words Cut 'n' Dye were embroidered just above it. Never had the salon's name been more apt.

Mr Edgar looked as if he were asleep, like his customer, but he wasn't dreaming of kids. He wasn't dreaming of anything at all: he was dead.

Until that day, life had been kind to Jefferson and shielded him. He'd never witnessed such a terrible scene before, and his reaction was spectacular. He

started to choke, then he made a strange sound that went something like, 'Waaaaagh . . . waaaaagh!'

That roughly translates as, 'Oh my gosh! This is a terrible sight!'

He went on with: 'Guhhhhhh-arghhhhh!' which meant something like, 'This man doesn't appear to have died of natural causes. In my opinion, this is a clear-cut case of murder.'

And he concluded with a drawn-out, plaintive 'Graaaaaaaaaaaah!'

In other words: 'A sight like this certainly shakes you up!'

Then he did the one thing he should never have done: he knelt down beside the body and whispered: 'Hold on there, Mr Edgar, I'm going to remove these . . .' as he grasped the scissors in his right hand and pulled them out of the wound, surprised at how hard they resisted. You'd think a blade plunged into a body would come out like a knife from butter, but that's not true – it sticks!

That was the moment the sleeping nanny goat chose to emerge from her sweet dream. What she saw – in other words Mr Edgar's body on the floor and beside him the murderer, weapon in hand – left her without the shadow of a doubt. She opened her enormous mouth and let out a shriek so shrill that one of the hand mirrors cracked: 'Eeeeeeeeee! Help! Eeeeeee! Murderer!'

Jefferson dropped the scissors. 'No, madam, it's not me! I came in and I—'

She wouldn't let him finish. She screamed all the louder, making the uvula at the back of her throat wobble. 'He's killed Mr Edgar! He's going to kill me too! Eeeeeeeeee!'

Jefferson pressed his hands together. 'No, madam, I swear—'

She pushed up the hood and tore off the plastic cap, exposing her mauve hair and her head full of curlers. Then she ran to the door and frantically yanked the handle, but the door was locked. She didn't hesitate. The certainty that she was trapped in a cramped room in the company of a killer gave her an energy rush. She took a two-metre run-up and charged, shoulder first, like a rugby pro. The door gave way immediately. The goat landed on the pavement on all four legs, bounced up as if she were mounted on springs and set off as fast as her short limbs would carry her.

She was shrieking non-stop. 'It's him! It's *hiiiiiiiiiiiim*!' pointing an accusing finger at Jefferson, who was standing in the doorway stammering feebly, 'No, no, it wasn't me!' much too softly to compete with the goat's ear-piercing screams.

When he saw that she'd already managed to alert two young billy goats, and they were making a beeline for him, trotting at first, then breaking into a run, he obeyed the oldest reflex in the world: flight. In other words, he cleared off, he scarpered, he skedaddled, or whatever you want to call it. Never in his life had he sprinted like that. He felt his legs spinning under him like the wheels of a racing car. Fear gave him wings, and he really did feel as if he was flying as he leaped over a sign saying *ROAD WORKS* and then a hole at least three metres wide. His pursuers had to skirt around it, which gave him a decisive lead. One of them yelled: 'Stop, Jefferson!' but on he ran, without letting up, turning right at each street corner so as to throw them off.

Instinct, combined with, it has to be said, a huge stroke of luck, led him to a patch of wasteland. There, hidden from view, he could at last slow down. He went to ground against a fence overgrown with nettles and brambles, his heart about to burst, his lungs on fire. He realised that during his flight, he'd been stammering continuously: 'It wasn't me, it wasn't me!'

He fell silent, waited a few minutes and, when he had fully recovered his breath, repeated, 'It wasn't me.'

Then he noticed his trousers were wet again, and this time it wasn't ditch water. The accident must have happened when he discovered the dead body. You have to understand – the shock, the emotion of it all. He almost wept with shame.

What would Chuck have done in his situation? The question had barely formed in his mind when the answer came: Chuck wouldn't have got himself into such a situation.

Jefferson risked a peek through a gap in the fence and saw that the countryside was very close. No way could he expose himself by walking along the road. He just needed to reach that clump of hazelnut trees, for example, and then he'd cut across the fields and go through the wood. Once home, he'd reflect on his situation. The most urgent thing was to find a safe place where he could think. He gave himself a pep talk, saying: 'Come on, hedgehog, be strong!' and he squeezed between two slats.

Less than twenty minutes later, the back of his house at the end of the forest path was already in view. Then his phone began to vibrate in his pocket. The cheerful face of Gilbert the pig appeared on the screen, then the text message:

16

Hey buddy, don't no where you are but I sujjest you
don't go home

Reading as he walked, Jefferson stopped in his
tracks and messaged:

But I'm almost home. I'll be there in a sec

The reply came back instantly:

Keep away, wotever you do! Turn around, go and
hyde in the woods and wait til I

Jefferson had no idea why Gilbert hadn't had time
to finish his sentence, but the message was clear: he'd
better not hang around. So he turned on his heel and
went back the way he'd come. Being told not to go
home because it's dangerous is very upsetting, because
there's no place safer than home. What could be the
threat? The police, already? He gave a few desperate
groans of 'Oh no, oh no', and walked slowly, ready to
dive into the undergrowth at the first warning.

The day had begun so well but now it was turning
into a nightmare. Starting with the horror of the hair

salon, nice Mr Edgar stabbed in the chest with his own scissors, Sophie missing, and worst of all: that stupid nanny goat who hadn't even given him two seconds to explain. He was the designated, obvious, unquestionable culprit, and his running away made him look guilty. The goat had seen him with her own eyes, she'd seen him holding the weapon, and besides, the crime squad would quickly find the fingerprints on the scissors and establish that they were his. The next day, his photo would be on the front page of *The Daily Trumpet* with an attention-grabbing headline in big letters: MURDERER!

The article would be just as incriminating:

Hedgehog Jefferson Ponsonby-Smythe killed the highly respected badger Mr Edgar on the premises of his hair salon Cut 'n' Dye. The motive for this brutal act is a mystery. The murderer fled.

He had reached this damning conclusion when his phone vibrated again. Gilbert! If reassurance was to be had from anywhere, it would be from him. They'd been friends since childhood, like brothers, more than brothers, because they had chosen each other.

The message read:

Hey buddy . . . here I am as promised: meet around
13:00 at the Cross, all right?

Jefferson, who had been stressing for over two
hours, felt a mixture of relief and emotion. Good
old Gilbert, you could count on him! He replied at
once: *OK*, then added:

*Oh, and three things: 1) bring me a spare pair of
trousers 2) don't ask me why 3) don't ask me why you
mustn't ask why.*

Then he sped up his pace. The Cross was at the
intersection of two paths, a few minutes away.

But as he made his way, feeling invigorated, he
began to have doubts. At first it was a little warning
bell, a barely perceptible *ding ding* . . . There was
something odd about Gilbert's message. He stopped
and re-read it carefully. The 'Hey buddy' was Gilbert's
usual greeting, and was credible, but the rest bothered
him. Gilbert would certainly not have written '13:00'
but rather '1 pm'. And that 'all right' at the end

wasn't like him either. He would have written 'OK' or 'okay'. Weird . . .

Uncertain, Jefferson decided to play smart. If Gilbert's phone was in the wrong hands, those of the police, for example, he needed to find out. He typed:

The Cross? You mean the place where we buried marbles when we were kids?

The reply came back less than thirty seconds later:

Yes, where we entombed them. See ya!

Then the little warning bell became a deafening alarm, with a built-in siren. First of all because Jefferson and Gilbert had never buried any marbles at that spot – he'd just made that up – and secondly because of the law of probabilities. You can accept the most unlikely occurrences: that the same person wins the Lottery three times in a row, or that the Pope takes up skipping, but there was one thing that was absolutely impossible, and that was that Gilbert the pig would use a literary word like entombed! His spelling was atrocious and that correctly spelled 'entombed' with the silent 'b', was beyond him. As for that pathetic 'See ya!' intended to sound young and cool, it didn't fool him: no way had Gilbert written that message.

Panicked by this discovery (but proud of himself for making it!), Jefferson decided to continue on to the Cross. He'd see who was there. In the meantime, he wouldn't send any more text messages which would immediately reveal his whereabouts. That's how so many criminals had been caught. You might as well wear a high-vis jacket, grab a megaphone and shout: 'I'm here, I'm here!'

When he was a stone's throw from the Cross, he turned off the path and slipped silently and furtively among the tall ferns.

The midnight-blue uniforms stood out from the green foliage, and in the nick of time Jefferson spotted the unmoving backs of two police officers lying in wait. Two Great Danes of course, because the crime squad was almost exclusively made up of that breed. Batons and handcuffs dangled from their belts. He hadn't been mistaken, the message was indeed a trap. A trap he had brilliantly thwarted. He veered to the right and spied another police officer hidden behind a dead tree, and then another. How many of those burly athletes had been sent to capture

Jefferson? He was all of 72 centimetres tall (with his heel cushions), and innocent to boot.

If they'd placed Gilbert as bait at the foot of the Cross, he wasn't going to walk into the lions' den to check. But if they'd let him go free, how on earth was he to find his friend now?

Jefferson had a little idea. And, with a bit of luck, the same thing would occur to Gilbert. The two of them had built a hut out of branches in a remote part of the woods. That had been seven or eight years ago when Jefferson was a very young hedgehog, still wet behind the ears, and Gilbert an immature young piglet. They'd worked hard on their hut for several months; it was a real labour of love. It had become their refuge, their secret hiding place. They'd spluttered over their first cigarette there, made themselves sick drinking cheap whisky and chilled listening to wild-boar rap (the best). They'd slept, eaten, laughed themselves silly and solved the world's problems there. If there was a hiding place where they could always go in the event of trouble, without even needing to tell each other, it was not the foot of the Cross – ha, ha! What a joke – but their hut!

Jefferson had no difficulty finding the hut, because his legs knew the way on their own, from sheer force of habit, but he had a shock on reaching it. The roof had caved in, the sides had collapsed, and the interior was overrun with brambles. And worst of all: Gilbert wasn't there. Jefferson checked his phone: it was 2.15 pm. He realised he was starving hungry and very thirsty. He sat down on a tree trunk, feeling pretty wretched.

'I should never have run away,' he said to himself. 'I should have pinned that hysterical nanny goat to the floor before she kicked down the door and called the police myself. I'm going to hand myself in. That's it, I'm going to hand myself in and explain what really happened.' He began to work out what he would say, out loud, with all the conviction he could muster: *'The first thing I saw was Mr Edgar's feet, you see, I moved forward a little . . . I kneeled down and . . . this lady goat was asleep, she didn't see anything . . . I don't hold it against her, you know, she honestly thought that . . . but I swear to you . . . why would I have done that? . . . I was very fond of Mr Edgar . . . he's always . . .'*

So went his confused reasoning as he talked to the empty forest around him, when suddenly he heard a rustling sound coming from some bushes nearby. He threw himself onto his stomach. Then came three little whistled notes, brief and high-pitched: *wh* . . .

whoo . . . whooo . . . reassured him. He answered back: *wh . . . whoo . . . whooo . . .* Their secret code. Gilbert!

Gilbert was taller than Jefferson, but that wasn't saying much. The striking thing about him was his incredibly radiant, happy-pig face. Jefferson would often say to himself that he had never seen anyone with such a gift for joyfulness. A sort of Olympic champion of cheeriness, a champion who didn't even need to train because that was his nature.

'What's this circus?' he laughed. 'I got picked up by three policemen staking out your place earlier. They asked me who I was and I told them—'

'Hold on,' Jefferson broke in. 'I'll tell you the whole story. But first of all, give me that.'

'Oh, yes. Here. They're mine. The legs will be a bit long on you, but you can just roll up the bottoms. Note that I'm not asking any questions and I'm not even smirking, OK. Look, am I smirking? No.'

He kept a straight face for three seconds before bursting out laughing. Jefferson shrugged.

'I got your message this morning, but I wasn't planning to come and see you, I was up to my ears in the *Highway Code*,' Gilbert went on, holding out the trousers that had been rolled up under his arm, and he tactfully turned his back so that Jefferson could get changed. 'Do you know that on a roundabout you must stay in the left-hand lane if you intend to turn—?'

Jefferson remembered that after years of missed buses, broken-down scooters and getting about on foot, his friend had made up his mind to take his driving test, a bold ambition because he was extremely clumsy and it was hard to imagine him at the wheel of anything other than a dodgem car.

'I'm sorry, Gilbert,' he interrupted him, 'but I'm not really thinking about roundabouts right now . . . The police took your phone, didn't they?'

'Yes, I told them I was your friend, so of course, as soon as they saw me typing a message, they confiscated it, the dogs! But they gave it straight back to me so I could arrange to meet you. They forced me. Only I'm not stupid, I twigged your trick with the marbles and I purposely used a very grown-up word to alert you.'

'Entombed?'

'Yes, that's right. I just made up the spelling. So, why are they after you?'

Faced with the enormity of what he was about to tell him, Jefferson hesitated. He finished doing up the trousers, threw the other pair behind a bush and

led his friend over to a moss-covered tree trunk, inviting him to sit down beside him.

'Gilbert, I . . . I've been accused of murder.'

Since he'd just been rehearsing, it wasn't too hard for him to describe the terrible chain of events that had led to him standing before Mr Edgar's lifeless body. He sobbed as he recalled the scissors planted in the good man's heart.

'Oh dear . . .' said Gilbert. 'A badgercide . . .'

Jefferson continued with the account of his frenzied flight. 'I'm going to turn myself in. Come with me. I'm going to turn myself in,' he ended, whispering into his handkerchief.

Gilbert had listened without laughing, for once. But in the silence that followed, he slowly shook his head from right to left, a blissful smile on his lips, as if in wonder, then he blurted out a surprising and most unexpected, 'Brill-iant!'

'What's brilliant?'

'I mean it's brilliant, isn't it? Thrilling! Think about it! For years we've been dreaming about something amazing happening to us, for years we've been making up stupid adventures, playing make-believe. And now, this is it! A real adventure!'

Jefferson hadn't really thought about his situation in that light.

'Are you mad or what?' he groaned. 'Can't you see! I'm going to be hanged, beheaded, shot. Maybe all three at once!'

'Stop it, Jeff. Have you forgotten that the death penalty's been abolished? At worst you'll get thirty years. It soon passes. I'll wait for you at the prison gates with a bunch of dandelions and a Zimmer frame.'

'Gilbert, I'm not in the mood for laughing.'

'OK. No more joking. But you mustn't turn yourself in.'

'Why not?'

'Because if they have to choose between believing you, my dearest little hedgehog, or believing that respectable nanny goat, they won't hesitate. I can see only one solution.'

'What's that?'

'You must hide and see how the investigation progresses. We'll rebuild the hut and you will sleep here. Tonight I'll bring you a blanket and something to eat. Come on, let's get to work!'

Without waiting for a reply, he started reconstructing the framework out of branches. He kept muttering little 'brill-iants' and Jefferson had no option but to help him.

When the hut's frame was more or less finished, they cleared away the brambles, threw armfuls of ferns over the roof and made four walls from leafy branches.

'There you are, Mr Jefferson! Like in the good old days! Stay hidden in here and wait for me. I'll be back before nightfall. I'll leave you my jacket in case I'm held up and the weather turns cold. We can forget about the phone, of course. And don't worry, OK? We'll prove your innocence.'

After about twenty metres, he turned around to add, still smiling, 'I'm sorry about Mr Edgar, by the way. He was a decent guy, wasn't he?'

Jefferson didn't doubt his friend's sincerity. He knew him well enough to be aware that with Gilbert, sadness sometimes took on a strange disguise.

He filled his afternoon as best he could. He washed his trousers in a stream and spread them on a rock to dry. He made the hut more comfortable by dragging in the stump that had served as a stool, then he improvised a mattress out of moss and leaves. But darkness fell over the wood without the tip of Gilbert's snout reappearing and he had to resign himself to curling up on his makeshift bed, wrapped in his friend's protective jacket and wondering what was going to become of him. He fell asleep, beset by confused thoughts of bloodstained scissors and an abandoned dish of creamy potatoes.

3

At dawn, he woke up cold, ravenous and shivering. It took him a few moments to remember where he was and why. His stomach immediately contracted into a hard ball. He was a criminal wanted by the police. He, whose worst offence had been to pilfer three caramel sweets from his village grocery when he was still a baby hedgehog! It was enough to drive a creature mad. He told himself once again that he ought to turn himself in. As soon as Gilbert came back, they'd go to the police station together and he would give himself up.

Meanwhile, he set off in search of some berries to stave off his hunger, but he found only three shrivelled blueberries that merely stained his fingers. He ventured as far as the stream to drink some water and wash his face. Back at the hut, he rummaged in his bag and was pleasantly surprised to find *Alone on the River*, which he'd forgotten to give Gilbert the previous day.

He idly flicked through it and came across the part where Chuck wakes up to find a huge tarantula sitting on his chest, beneath his shirt. Scared witless, he doesn't move but talks softly to the giant spider: 'Please, tarantula, please don't hurt me.' After an anxious hour, he realises it's asleep, that it's nice and warm against him and it feels good there. He moves the tarantula bit by bit so as not to wake it, and, once he's removed it from his chest, he runs around like a madman shouting with the joy that he's still alive. Reading that passage made Jefferson feel brave again. After all, there was no tarantula asleep on him – or at least not for now.

Gilbert appeared just as the first ray of sunlight filtered through the branches of the beech trees. He was trotting towards the hut, an overnight bag slung over his shoulder and brandishing a copy of *The Daily Trumpet* in his right hand.

'Jeff, Jeff! You're famous!'

Jefferson tore the newspaper from him and unfolded it, convinced his picture would be on the front page, but it wasn't. There was simply a photo of the hair salon with the chalk outline of Mr Edgar's body on the floor. A huge headline ran right across the top of the page: *MURDER AT CUT 'N' DYE.* The only face shown, in a smaller picture, was that of the nanny goat, without her curlers, her features ravaged by emotion and four microphones thrust under her goatee.

'Do you want to read first or eat? I've brought you three Danish pastries, three almond croissants and three bananas. I tried to make it balanced. And I've even got a Thermos full of hot cocoa with lots of sugar! How's that?'

Jefferson, who hadn't had eaten a thing for twenty-four hours, felt weak on listening to the menu.

'Give it here and read me the article while I eat, please.'

They sat down on the same mossy tree trunk as the previous day and Gilbert unwrapped the pastries which were a bit squashed in their little paper bag from the bakery. Jefferson devoured a Danish pastry voraciously, with the excuse that peeling a banana would take him too long.

'Right, I'll read it to you,' said Gilbert:

Yesterday morning, at around 10 o'clock, our town's police station received a call from Mrs Kristiansen, nanny goat, in connection with a serious crime at the hair salon Cut 'n' Dye located in Topp St. On arrival at the scene, the police, dogs, could only establish the death of the hairdresser, Mr Edgar, badger. He appeared to have been stabbed with a pair of scissors, left at the salon by the killer. Mrs Kristiansen (see below) alleges that the murderer is the young J.P.S., hedgehog, who apparently fled the scene once he'd done the deed.

'And what does this lady say?'
'Wait, I'm getting to it. So . . . yes, she says . . .'

I was frightened out of my wits. I saw him stab Mr Edgar with the scissors. At least five times. I screamed as loudly as I could, then he stared at me and snarled and I realised that he was going to attack me too. I managed to run away, but I'm still shaking all over. That creature—

'But she's bleating utter nonsense!' choked Jefferson,

spitting out a mouthful of cocoa. 'It's pure lies. She has no right!'

'I don't know whether she has the right,' replied Gilbert, 'but readers are likely to believe her. The baker's wife is reminding all her customers about that serial killer who murdered several people. What was his name?'

'Alex Vral? But that was in the nineteenth century! And he was as mad as a hatter!'

'Yes, I'll say, completely out of his mind. He signed his murders by writing his name with his victims' intestines. But all the same, he was a hedgehog. Sorry, Jeff. And that's what folk are like. They'll say it's in the blood. Another thing, my friend, and this will make your spikes stand on end, let me warn you: this Mrs Kristiansen is the wife of Judge Kristiansen, you know, that billy goat who's easy-going on animals with horns and tough on the others. And no matter how hard I look, you don't have horns . . .'

'Oh no,' snivelled Jefferson, biting into his second croissant.

His plan to turn himself in now seemed a lot less wise. He would have no chance of giving his version of events. Gilbert read his thoughts.

'Listen, hedgehog, I've thought long and hard and here's my idea: the only way to prove your innocence is for us to arrest the killer ourselves and hand him over to the police. What do you think?'

'But Gilbert, we're not detectives! And besides, I daren't show my face anywhere. By tomorrow my picture will be all over the town with "WANTED" on it. Suddenly, I've lost my appetite,' he added, throwing the skin of his third banana over his shoulder.

'Just as well,' said Gilbert, 'seeing as you've eaten everything! Now don't lose hope. There's some good news inside the paper: Sophie wasn't at the salon yesterday morning. She's got laryngitis and had taken the day off. Her illness may have saved her life.'

Jefferson merely gave a half-hearted nod. He didn't want to lay bare his innermost feelings for the young badger, not even to his best friend. But he was hugely relieved to learn that she was out of harm's way. That is probably why he didn't immediately say no to Gilbert's crazy idea of conducting the investigation themselves.

'Of course you can't show your face in town,' Gilbert went on. 'But I've thought of everything. Ta da! Drumroll: you will go in disguise.'

'In disguise! Are you out of your mind! Disguised as what? Can you see me as a sheep, a turkey or a dragonfly?'

'Nothing of the sort. As your *sister*.'

'Sorry?'

By way of a reply, Gilbert opened the overnight bag and fished out a pile of random clothes: there was a white calf-length skirt with bright yellow trimming, a sky-blue blouse, a pair of pumps and a blonde wig, as well as a handbag and a little washbag.

'But that's Chelsea's stuff!' squealed Jefferson on recognising his sister's clothes.

'I just told you. I popped into her place and told her everything. She's amazing, your sister, I promise you. She didn't hesitate for a moment. Even better, you're the same size!'

Jefferson was dumbstruck at first, then, screwing up his eyes, he muttered, 'No way would I wear my sister's clothes, not even for a quarter of a thousandth of a millionth of a second.'

'Fine,' Gilbert said. 'I shan't insist.'

He picked up the bag and vanished inside the hut for ages. Jefferson heard him moving around inside, amid the rustle of fabric, punctuated by the occasional curse. Then came a zipping sound, and at last the leafy curtain parted and the creature who appeared before him literally took his breath away.

'Yes, I dropped into your sister's, and to mine as well!' Gilbert informed him, imitating a girl's voice. 'What do you imagine? They're watching me too! My best friend's a murderer, for goodness sake . . .'

He was wearing a red lace dress, stockings, heels and a curly wig. And he'd emphasised his eyes with eyeliner.

Then Jefferson, who since the previous day had been a bundle of nerves and anxiety, started laughing hysterically and couldn't stop. Each time he managed to calm down a little, one look at Gilbert was enough to set him off again.

'I'm sorry, it's nerves . . .'

The conversation was fraught. Partly because Gilbert's idea was crazy, and partly because a crazy idea coming from a boy dressed as a girl sounds doubly crazy.

'You see, Jeff, the logical thing would be for us to visit the crime scene to search for clues, but unfortunately only real police officers can do that, and not amateurs like us. We have to . . . can you stop laughing when I'm talking to you?'

'Sorry, but the minute I look at you . . . Could you at least take off the wig?'

'OK. I was saying, that since we can't go to Cut 'n' Dye, we'll have to set about it differently. We need to find the motive for the murder. Mr Edgar wasn't killed for no reason. The most important thing is to find out more about him to have some understanding of this case. And seeing as he's no longer here to answer our questions, I thought of Sophie. The problem is, we don't know where she lives.'

'*I* do.'

'You know? How? Did you follow her?'

'No! Well, yes, sort of . . . just a little, out of curiosity, from a distance . . .'

'I see . . .'

'You don't see anything at all.'

Jefferson was certain there was no chance that Sophie would agree to see them, but Gilbert was determined. He had a little idea.

When they set out, at around ten o'clock in the morning, after concealing all their male clothing inside the hut, anyone out for a stroll who met them by chance would have taken them for two innocent girls going for a walk.

They entered the town with hesitant steps, especially Gilbert whose high heels were a size too small and were pinching his big toe. As they crossed the park, two young pigs perched on the back of a bench stared at them unashamedly and wolf-whistled them as they passed.

'It's really horrible!' complained Jefferson without turning around. 'I had no idea. I won't do *that* any more.'

'But you never did,' Gilbert pointed out.

'True. So let's say I never will.'

4

Sophie lived in a charming little apartment building close to the town centre. Her name was on her letter box which also indicated that she lived on the third floor. They took the lift and, as they went up, Gilbert advised Jefferson to say as little as possible if she let them in. Sophie was likely to recognise the young hedgehog's voice, whereas he, Gilbert, would be more comfortable steering the conversation.

On the landing, they adjusted each other's clothing, which set Jefferson off giggling again. Gilbert knocked. They heard a hoarse cough – *cough! Cough!* – and footsteps, and they guessed that someone was looking at them through the peephole.

'What do you want? Who are you?' said a voice muffled by laryngitis and the heavy door.

'We're two young interns from *The Daily Trumpet*,'

replied Gilbert in what he believed to be a girl's voice, 'and we'd like to talk to you for a few minutes.'

'I have nothing to say to you. I'm ill. *Cough!*'

Gilbert had foreseen this reaction and had prepared his counter-attack.

'The thing is, we don't want people spreading rumours about Mr Edgar. Your testimony is important, Miss. You're his niece and you know him well. And because we're interns at the paper, like you at the salon, I believe . . .'

Gilbert winked at Jefferson. He'd just used his secret ploy. *We young interns need to support one another, right?*

'I'm ill,' Sophie repeated.

There was a brief silence and then, 'All right. But only a few minutes. And no photos.'

'Promise!' said Gilbert, jubilant.

They very quickly understood the reason for this last request. The Sophie who opened the door to them bore little resemblance to the smart, well-groomed Sophie of the hair salon. She was in her dressing-gown and slippers, her hair dishevelled, and no make-up. Her eyes were red, probably as much from illness as from grief. And her voice sounded a bit like that of a young donkey learning to bray, without much success. That didn't stop Jefferson from finding her charming. It was a charm that was less obvious and more endearing, that's all.

'Do you want to see our press cards?' asked Gilbert as soon as they were inside.

Jefferson jumped. What had got into him, the idiot, being so over-zealous when he hadn't been asked?

'Yes, I would,' replied Sophie. 'I'm sorry, but – *cough!* – you're right, I'd rather be certain.'

They both began rummaging in their handbags while she went to fetch a tissue from the coffee table in the sitting room. Jefferson glared daggers at his friend. Messing up an investigation in three seconds, before it had even begun? Smart move. They may as well turn tail (literally) and go home!

They were saved by Sophie's phone, which started ringing just as she came back in, blowing her nose. She made an apologetic gesture and moved away to answer it. All the same, they heard her saying thank you and repeating several times that she was fine, that there was no need to worry about her.

A female friend, most likely.

'I have to go,' she said at last. 'I've got two young trainee journalists from *The Daily Trumpet* here.'

Perhaps they really had managed to convince her that they were novice reporters! In any case, miraculously, she didn't bring up the matter of their press cards again. It had slipped her mind.

'Do sit down,' she invited, indicating a floral sofa. 'And don't take any notice of the mess.'

That's what obsessively tidy people usually say. Sophie's place was immaculate and Jefferson was aware of it. The two visitors seated themselves side-by-side and realised how difficult it was to sit down when wearing a skirt or dress. *Should I cross my legs? Shouldn't I?* They decided to press their knees together and rest their notebooks on them.

'Right,' began Gilbert. 'Please tell us about your uncle.'

'Oh, my uncle Edgar . . . He was a . . .'

She was tongue-tied. It was probably too soon to acknowledge his death and talk about him. Only a few hours had gone by since the tragedy, and the poor young lady had probably not slept a wink that night.

'He was a calm man . . . Reassuring. Just imagine, he'd been running his – *cough!* – salon for over forty years. He always used to say that he was "well established", which is important for a hairdresser. He liked making jokes, which sometimes fell flat, but they made him laugh. He'd guffaw into his double chin and we – *cough! cough!* – we'd laugh at the sound of him laughing. One day, one of his customers . . .'

The more she talked, the more she told them and the more Jefferson wanted to tear off his wig and own up to their scheme. He felt uncomfortable deceiving people in general, and Sophie especially. Gilbert, on the other hand, had no such qualms. He encouraged her to carry on, making approving *hmm*s, and scribbled frantically in his notebook. Jefferson, sitting beside him, saw that in fact he wasn't writing anything at all but was jotting down random words of no interest: *car, arrive, a lot* . . . or even gobbledegook: *fatshterke . . . sjeondasdheb . . .*

Sophie's phone rang again. She glanced at the screen and jumped up.

'Excuse-me. It's my aunt.'

This time, she disappeared into the kitchen, but the two imposters could hear her broken voice: 'Yes, auntie, I'm fine . . . no, I couldn't sleep . . . you neither, I imagine . . . *cough, cough, cough!* . . . no, auntie, I haven't heard anything more . . . no, there's no point . . . yes, auntie . . . I know . . . I know . . . *cough, cough!* . . . yes, me too . . .'

Jefferson had already noticed that people who

46

are very upset sometimes hold back their tears for a long time, but then the floodgates open as soon as they talk to someone. And the more they love the person they are talking to, the more copiously they weep. According to this principle, he said to himself, Sophie must be very fond of her aunt. A tear came to his eyes, out of empathy, a simple little sob, and Gilbert dug him hard in the ribs to remind him of his role: a journalist doesn't cry in front of his interviewees.

When Sophie came back to join them in the sitting room, she seemed even more grief-stricken than before. She sat down and took a tablet with a sip of water.

'That was my aunt.'

They said nothing for a moment, and then Gilbert, like a true professional, resumed the interview, 'Everything that you are telling us, Miss, suggests that your uncle had few enemies, which makes us wonder—'

'Few enemies? He didn't have *any*! No, I think that hedgehog was simply in the grip of a . . . *cough! Cough!* . . . the grip of a killing frenzy. Forgive me, Miss,' she went on addressing Jefferson, 'I know one shouldn't generalise. And I'm not. But all the same –

cough! – everyone remembers that hedgehog, that monster who murdered eight people . . .'

'Alex Vral,' retorted Gilbert. 'Now look, that was last century and he was a lunatic!'

'Yes, of course, of course. But otherwise how can you explain it? I don't understand it at all. Several hedgehogs were customers at the salon and I liked them all, but that one, I mean the one who's accused of the murder, that Mr Jefferson, well . . . it's a terrible thing to say . . .'

'Yes?' encouraged Gilbert.

'I have to admit that . . . I was especially . . . fond of him.'

Gilbert glance covertly at his journalist colleague with a faint smile. Sophie bowed her head and sobbed even more profusely. Jefferson was utterly confused. It was like a classical tragedy: the hero (Jefferson) is wrongly accused of having killed the uncle (Edgar) of the woman he loves (Sophie), but learns the following day, disguised as a girl, that she is not indifferent to his charms. What a muddle! It was enough to make him both delighted and dejected. In a nutshell, he felt completely out of his depth and merely bowed his head and concentrated on his notebook.

But dejected, Gilbert most certainly wasn't.

'Tell me, Miss, I understand your grief and your anger, but supposing the investigation proves that this young hedgehog, presumed innocent, really *is* innocent, would you then . . . ?'

That was when everything started to go wrong. Sophie was sniffing pathetically and Gilbert leaned forward to grab a tissue from the box on the coffee table. As he reached out, he knocked over the glass of water and let out a manly: 'Damn!' Sophie looked up, alarmed at this sudden deep voice. Gilbert straightened up abruptly but this rapid movement dislodged his wig. The fringe slid round to the side of his head and the curls tumbled over his eyes.

Sophie opened her mouth wide. 'What on earth . . . ?'

Then Jefferson decided that this had gone on long enough. He couldn't bear it any more. He slowly raised his hand to his own wig and snatched it off his head, freeing his quiff which stood on end.

Sophie leaped up and shrieked as if she'd seen a ghost. 'Nooooo! Mr Jefferson! Noooooo!'

'Please,' he entreated, 'don't be frightened. I . . . I'm not dangerous.'

She choked, white as a sheet, looking around to see how she could escape should he attack her.

'I swear I didn't kill your uncle. Let me explain,' entreated Jefferson. To look at him, it would be hard to imagine him killing anything other than time.

Eventually she sat down again, exhausted by her fever and all the emotion. The two friends also sat back down. Gilbert held out the tissue that had set the whole thing off, while Jefferson went into the kitchen to find a sponge to mop up the water on the coffee table. Then he refilled Sophie's glass.

'Here. Drink some water and listen to us. We're going to tell you the whole story.'

He told her about his terrible discovery at Cut 'n' Dye and how he'd run away. He was practised at it now, and he sounded so convincing that it was impossible not to believe him. Gilbert continued, telling her about their woodland hideout and their decision to conduct the investigation themselves. She listened to them open-mouthed and, when they'd finished, she gave a deep sigh.

'Common sense – *cough!* – tells me that I should call the police at once and hand you over, but there's something stopping me, and it's . . .'

At that point she had an even longer coughing fit that was painful to listen to: *cough! Cough! Cough! Cough! Cough! Cough!* She had turned scarlet, with sweat pouring off her, and she had to wipe her face before continuing. 'It's that . . . I believe you. And I think you're so brave. Unfortunately I fear that Mrs Kristiansen's testimony will carry a lot of weight and, what's more, her husband is none other than . . . *cough!*'

'We know, Miss Sophie,' Gilbert broke in to relieve her, 'and that's why we want to find the murderer ourselves. The problem is that we know nothing, or almost nothing, about Mr Edgar. We need something to go on in order to start the investigation, you see. Is there nothing in his life that's . . . I don't know . . . that's less than squeaky clean?'

She thought long and hard.

'There is in fact something – *cough!* – but it's probably of no importance and I hesitate to . . .'

'Please!' they chorused.

'Well, it's this – *cough!* – the salon is closed on Mondays.'

This revelation didn't seem earth-shattering and the two friends waited for what was to follow.

'That's to say . . . how can I put it . . . ? My uncle used to disappear every Monday.'

'What do you mean, "used to disappear"?' they asked in surprise, again in perfect harmony.

'Well, for the past two years, he was in the habit of taking the train every Sunday and only coming back on Tuesday morning when the salon opened.'

'Oh. And where did he go?'

'No one knows. It was his – *cough!* – secret.'

'Is it possible, I mean, did Mr Edgar, with all due respect, of course, might he have had a lady fr—' began Jefferson.

'Right,' interrupted Gilbert. 'It's not much to go on, but it's a start. Listen, Miss Sophie, we're going to let you rest and take care of that cough. You badly need to. Thank you very much for agreeing to see us despite your loss. We're going to do our utmost to make headway with the investigation, aren't we Jefferson?'

Jefferson agreed. They rose and went over to the door.

'Good – *cough! Cough!* – good luck!' spluttered Sophie, but as they were about to open the door, she called them back.

'Wait, I . . . I may be wrong, but I can't help trusting you. I'm listening to my intuition. And there's something – *cough! Cough! Cough!* – I'd like to show you.'

She turned on her heel and vanished into what

must have been her bedroom, returning a few moments later with an envelope in her hand. She held it out to Jefferson.

'Here. You can open it later. My uncle liked travelling and, wherever he went on holiday, he'd send me a postcard. He didn't have any children and I'm his only niece, you see. This is the most recent card he sent me, only three weeks ago. It might – *cough! Cough! Cough!* – set you on the right track. I'll leave it with you, but please don't lose it and make sure you give it back as soon as you can. It's of great sentimental value to me.'

'Promise,' said Jefferson, touched that she'd entrusted the card to him rather than to Gilbert. It created something personal, almost *intimate*, between them.

He slipped it into his handbag.

'One last thing,' whimpered the poorly young badger with what little voice she had left, 'if you ever have to dress up as girls again, pay attention to your make-up because it's a complete . . . *cough! Cough!* . . . It's a complete disaster. You need to go easy on the foundation, because you look as if you've slapped on a load of peanut butter.'

They restyled their wigs in the lift and tried to

leave the building as naturally as possible. In the park, the flirtatious pigs, whose buttocks appeared to be glued to the bench, wolf-whistled them again.

'They bring shame on my species,' complained Gilbert. 'Why don't we go and punch their faces in? That would teach them a lesson, having their snouts flattened by a couple of girls.'

'Forget it,' hissed Jefferson, taking his arm and dragging him away. 'This is no time to draw attention to ourselves.'

That suited Gilbert fine. He hated fighting.

They crossed the rest of the town without incident, eager to be hidden from view. As soon as they were back in the wood, Gilbert took off his shoes and they started trotting along the path.

5

The postcard showed a city scene. An elegant footbridge spanned a canal lined with the brightly coloured façades of ancient houses. The trees with their autumn leaves were reflected in the water. Cyclists rode past.

'Lovely,' commented Gilbert. 'Very romantic. Do you recognise it?'

They were sitting on their tree trunk outside the hut, dressed in their own clothes. Jefferson shook his head.

'No. I'd say it's in the Land of the Humans, but where exactly . . .' He turned the card over. 'I'm right. It's Granville.'

'Granville? What's that?'

'It's a big city. Very touristy. With a beautiful cathedral, I think. A river, canals, bridges . . .'

'How do you know all that?'

'Because I didn't sit snoozing by the radiator in geography class, unlike *some* people.'

The stamp and postmark confirmed that the card had definitely been posted from Granville. Uncle Edgar had neat handwriting.

My dear Sophie,
I'm sending you this beautiful view of the city with my fondest wishes. You see what lovely things the humans are capable of making. ~~*Sadly, they can also*~~
See you soon, back home.
Love and kisses, your uncle Edgar.

They were both surprised at the crossed-out half-sentence which was still legible: ~~Sadly, they can also~~. Was it deliberate? Gilbert thought not. In his view, the uncle had been about to tell his niece something, then changed his mind, but because he'd already put a stamp on the card, he simply crossed out the sentence he'd begun. He'd done it in haste, without realising the words could still be read. That's all there was to it. Jefferson, on the other hand, thought that it had been deliberate. Mr Edgar was a perfectionist and was meticulous. If he'd really not wanted Sophie to read that half-sentence, he would have blanked it out properly or he'd simply have torn up the card and written another, without any crossings-out. He could afford the cost of a stamp. No, that was the act of a man who wanted to say something without saying it while *still* saying it!

They argued over the question for a while, without being able to make up their minds, until Jefferson suddenly froze.

'What is it?' asked Gilbert.

Jefferson was astounded at the workings of his own brain. It was as if a thought had made a long underwater voyage and now, stimulated by another, it rose to the surface and burst in a little bubble of evidence.

'The thing is, I've just remembered something. On the morning of the murder, I went into town on foot, as you know, and I was almost run over . . .'

He told Gilbert about the car driving at breakneck speed, the two humans inside, and his tumble into the ditch.

'Eighty miles an hour on a country road,' said Gilbert, outraged. 'The speed limit's fifty-five, *fifty* if the road's wet or if the driver has had a licence for less than—'

'Fine, Gilbert, you don't need to recite the *Highway Code* again. What strikes me is the coincidence: those two humans in the getaway car – because yes, on thinking about it, it did look like a getaway – and now this card sent by Mr Edgar from the Land of the Humans! Twice over, everything points to the humans in this affair, that's what I'm saying to myself.'

'Of course!' yelled Gilbert. 'Brill-iant! Absolutely brill-iant!'

He started capering about like a mountain goat.

'We're going to visit the humans! You're right: that's the key! Our investigation's moving forward! I love this! You know what? I think I'm going to stop training to be a central-heating engineer and become a detective!'

Jefferson suddenly remembered that at this hour he himself should have been sitting in the lecture theatre at the university where he was in his second year of a geography degree. Instead, he was hanging around in the woods, accused of murder, in the company of a flippant pig who was unaware of the danger. 'We're two fake journalists,' he said to himself, 'we're two fake detectives, but most of all we're two real idiots.'

Gilbert finished his madcap dance and sat back

down on the tree trunk. 'I'm going home to get all the things we'll need for the journey. And I'll buy the newspaper so we can cut out the photo of Mr Edgar. Then we can show it to people over there and—'

'One thing at a time, piglet!' said Jefferson, trying to calm him down. 'You're getting carried away and you're forgetting a few small details.'

'What, for instance?'

'For instance, that I can't go back home, that I don't have any spare clothes or a washbag. I don't even have any money. I'd just gone out to get my hair cut, remember. You're also forgetting that I'm the most wanted hedgehog in the land, so I can't see myself blithely taking the train, even in disguise, and . . .'

'You won't be disguised and we won't be taking the train, little hedgehog.'

'Oh, really? And how will we get there? By car? I don't drive, and you don't yet, thank heavens.'

'We won't be going by car!'

'On foot?'

'We won't be going on foot.'

Gilbert kept Jefferson on tenterhooks for a few seconds more, then announced calmly, 'We're going by coach.'

'By coach?'

'Yes. Because I've just had an amazing idea and even I'm blown away by it. If we hang around the city for our investigation, it won't be long before we're spotted by the humans. They'll think we're dodgy. So I thought about it long and hard and—'

'You thought long and hard . . . when?'

'Um, when I was dancing just now, even if I didn't look as if I was. And I've found the answer. Let's see if you're as smart as I am: what's the best way to travel when you want to go unnoticed?'

Since Jefferson was sulking, Gilbert answered the question himself. 'A package tour!'

'You want us to conduct our investigation on a package tour?'

'That's right! You go around in a herd, no one pays any attention to you, you take as many photos as you please. It's ideal. And it so happens that my cousin Roland works for a travel agency, Globetrotters – do you know it?'

Jefferson had often seen the yellow coaches that criss-crossed the country with a slogan on the back that had always fascinated him: *AVID FOR ADVENTURE? JOIN THE GLOBETROTTERS!*

'And what does your cousin do at Globetrotters?'

'He's a driver.'

'But, Gilbert, I can't budge from here. I'd get caught the minute I poked my snout outside this wood.'

'No. We'll sneak ourselves onto the coach. I'll sign you up under a false name. My cousin will arrange everything. Come on, I'm going to find out about the forthcoming trips. As for your things, we'll think of something when the time comes. Don't worry, I'll deal with it.'

Hyped up like that, Gilbert was unstoppable, but as he trotted off down the path, Jefferson called him back:

'Wait. That's twice I've forgotten.'

He opened his rucksack and pulled out *Alone on the River.*

'Here. I borrowed it from the library for you. It's the story of a boy called Chuck who . . . well, you'll see. I loved it. I think it's the best book I've ever read in my whole life.'

'That good?'

'That good.'

It so happened that Globetrotters had arranged a trip to Granville, in the Land of the Humans, for three days' time. Three days which Jefferson spent in and around the hut, waiting for Gilbert's visits. He slept a lot, washed in the stream, read a dozen novels and ate around thirty bananas and sixty pastries.

Each day, *The Daily Trumpet* brought a fresh stream of news about the murder. Mrs Kristiansen in particular was out of control. In one interview, she even said: *'His eyes were bloodshot and he was frothing at the mouth. He shouted: "Long live Alex Vral!" and rushed at me. The simple fact is, I had a miraculous escape . . .'*

Each edition featured a different photo of her. Sometimes she looked horror-struck, sometimes she was in tears, but always in a state of great elation.

Fortunately, Sophie offered a more balanced view:

'I understand Mrs Kristiansen's distress, but I cannot believe that Mr Jefferson is guilty. He was a particularly polite customer, much valued by everyone at Cut 'n' Dye. I hope with all my heart, and in the name of my uncle's memory, that light will soon be shed on what really happened.'

One morning, Jefferson had a shock. His photo was on the front page, and what a photo! They'd dug it out of their archive. He'd won a baking competition, six years earlier, and the photo showed him presenting his blueberry tart, an embarrassed smile on his face, but his quiff already defiant. How could anyone imagine for a moment that in the space of a few years, this sweet, timid hedgehog baker could become a bloodthirsty monster? The journalist pointed out this contradiction in his article, and, without directly challenging Mrs Kristiansen's account, he defended the principle that in the absence of proof and a confession, a presumed culprit must first and foremost be presumed innocent. Jefferson was grateful to him and promised himself he'd look him up and thank him when this whole business was nothing but a bad memory.

Although Gilbert lacked imagination when it came to food, he did excel when it came to their wardrobe, and he fitted them both out with trousers, summer shirts and an array of caps with visors. He included vital accessories such as sunglasses, a camera on a shoulder strap, and bumbags. He had a harder job convincing Jefferson that he'd have to sacrifice his quiff, which might give him away. At first, Jefferson refused adamantly. He'd worn his rebel cowlick with pride ever since nursery school and it had become as much a part of him as his head or his legs.

'Except that it'll grow back,' Gilbert had argued, 'and heads don't, as far as I'm aware.'

Unhappy but resigned, Jefferson eventually sat down on their tree trunk. Gilbert stood behind him, scissors in hand.

'Close your eyes and relax.'

He grabbed the quiff in his left hand and placed it between the scissor blades.

'Say: "Cut!" I want you to be the one to give the order.'

Jefferson felt tears welling up and, for fear of changing his mind, he immediately said a sad, 'Cut'.

One clack and the deed was done.

'Shall I show it to you?' asked Gilbert like a dentist after extracting a molar.

'No, throw it away,' replied Jefferson, glad there was no mirror in the hut. To see the top of his person thus shorn of its crowning glory would probably have upset him a great deal.

Given that it was a long journey to the Land of the Humans, the coach was scheduled to depart at the crack of dawn. Which was lucky for the two friends, who managed to reach the meeting point without encountering a soul on the way.

Over the past few days, Gilbert had tried to get into Jefferson's cottage, but it was still under surveillance and he had easily spotted the burly Great Danes who were not very skilled in the art of camouflage.

The little yellow coach was waiting in the car park behind the travel agency, the engine already running. Some fifteen holidaymakers were busy putting their suitcases in the luggage compartment, helped by Roland, who laughed at each bag or case. Cheerfulness seemed to be in the family's genes. As soon as he saw his cousin, Roland went over and embraced him, then he gave Jefferson an exaggerated wink as he shook his hand: 'Mr Sangalli, hello!'

'What is that stupid name?' asked Jefferson as soon as Roland was out of earshot.

'Sangalli? It's the name of the engineer who invented the radiator. He was a Russian and his name was spelled San Galli, I just changed it a little. So don't complain. You're very happy to just switch on your radiator in the winter instead of trying to light a fire with a piece of flint.'

They stowed their bags themselves and were

about to board the coach when a voice boomed, 'Oh, I say! You look just like the murderer, you do! All that's missing is the quiff, ha ha ha!'

Jefferson's heart began to pound. They hadn't even set off yet, and he'd already been recognised. It was a fat, ruddy-faced boar on stumpy legs who'd spoken, and he was in high spirits.

'Darling, don't you think he looks like Robertson ... um Williamson ... you, know, whatshisname ... that murderer fellow ...'

'Walter, stop it, you're not funny!' scolded his wife, who was also chubby and whose formidable bosom was bursting out of her blouse. Two of the buttons looked as if they were holding by a single thread, making Gilbert and Jefferson want to distance themselves from the threat.

Then Gilbert had a surprising reaction: with the utmost calm, he said, 'Yes, it's him all right. It's Jefferson! He'll have cut off his quiff so as to go unnoticed! Help, I'm frightened!'

A few travellers smiled and Jefferson tried to do likewise. Then the boar came up very close to him and said quietly, 'I'm sorry. I'm Schmitt. Walter Schmitt. It was a joke. I like cracking jokes. You won't hold it against me, I hope.'

He must have sprayed himself with eau de cologne for at least a minute. The scent was literally eye-watering.

'Of course not, I don't hold it against you,' replied Jefferson, telling himself to avoid Walter Schmitt for the entire trip.

'Thank you,' said the boar, shaking his hand. 'What about you, what's your name?'

'Um . . . Sangalli. I'm Mr Sangalli.'

They chose seats in the middle of the coach and watched those who would be their travel companions for the next ten days settle themselves down. Two quiet, lovey-dovey squirrels, an elderly sheep couple who helped each other into their seats, two conspiratorial, chattering vixens, ready to make fun of everyone as it seemed to Jefferson . . . He had mixed feelings on seeing a couple of stern-looking middle-aged badgers. They both wore a discreet black armband as a sign of mourning and he wondered how they would feel about the presence of a hedgehog, only a few days after the tragedy at Cut 'n' Dye. They sat in the front. Time would tell.

Then came a cow and two young calves and a fat Angora cat who sat right at the back against the window, his camera on his knee. Then a nanny goat

and her husband, a duck and even more passengers. Within a few minutes, the coach was almost full. The last to board was a thin, lanky female rabbit who was still young but dressed like a granny. She moved down the aisle mumbling shy 'hello's.

'Her name's Simone,' explained Gilbert, 'she's a bit miserable. She goes on all the trips to find a husband. If you're interested . . .'

Roland welcomed them all, assuring them that he would do his utmost to make their trip enjoyable. He asked whether they'd prefer to drive in silence or with the radio on. The two elderly sheep raised their hands in unison, most likely to say that they would like peace and quiet so they could go back to sleep, but the vixens beat them to it, 'The radio! Music!'

Roland sat down at the wheel and put on the local radio. From the early hours, it blared out a constant stream of chatter, ads for items whose price always ended in something-ninety-nine, and presenters interrupting one another talking nonsense. The coach manoeuvred out of the car park, drove through the sleeping town and set off down a country road. They passed the spot where Jefferson had almost been run over a few days earlier, then close to the path that led to his cottage. He had a lump in his throat. His dish of creamy potatoes must be burned to a cinder by now.

'Chin up, hedgehog,' whispered Gilbert, 'with a bit of luck, we'll be home in ten days with the murderer trussed up in the luggage compartment.'

With that, he put on his headphones and buried his snout in his *Highway Code*, which was open at the 'Signalling' section.

'*With a bit of luck . . .*' sighed Jefferson, opening the novel he was reading.

A strong whiff of eau de cologne was coming from behind him. He turned around and found himself nose-to-nose with the flushed face of Mr Schmitt, who was pushing his snout between the two seats.

'Apologies again for earlier.'

Yes, it was going to be a long journey.

6

Although he was fascinated by geography, Jefferson had never crossed the border and the thought gave him butterflies in his tummy. Leaving his familiar world behind made him uncomfortable, especially since he knew he was wanted. He could already picture himself being seized, arrested and flung to the ground with his hands twisted behind his back, handcuffed, tied up and taken back, and he imagined the headline of *The Daily Trumpet*: *Killer Jefferson Ponsonby-Smythe caught trying to flee the country under a false identity. We can breathe again.*

Fortunately, border checks were limited to the turnstiles of the impatient police officer on duty who said, 'Next, next!' as if they were of no importance and simply a nuisance. So they made it through and drove all morning on main roads lined with plane trees, traversing the occasional charmless small town or village, their noses glued to the windows all the same. The local inhabitants stared openly at them. Children pulled faces at them or tried to imitate them, it was hard to tell.

They stopped for lunch at a restaurant reserved exclusively for them, and then took the motorway, reaching Granville by nightfall. They were overawed by the height of the buildings, and it was odd seeing almost no one but humans in the bustling streets. Jefferson had never seen so many at once! Back home, in the Animal Kingdom, you'd meet them from time to time, visiting on business or as tourists, but they were the exceptions. Here, they had suddenly become the norm. And conversely, the passengers on the Globetrotters coach were the ones attracting attention.

At the Majestic Hotel, Jefferson had the feeling that the two receptionists were nudging each other and stifling a giggle as they checked them in. He studied his companions. Suitcases at their feet, they waited patiently to be given the keys to their rooms. He had to admit that the array of faces might make people smile: massive heads and wizened faces, some elongated skulls and others flat, dangling or pointed ears, horns, beaks and moustaches. He glanced at his own reflection in a mirror and saw his pointed snout, his round, beady eyes and shorn head. He had to admit that seen through human eyes . . .

At first, he made an effort not to judge humans too quickly. Preconceived opinions are dangerous, as he well knew!

But on the second morning, at breakfast, the following happened: Mr and Mrs Cousins, the two elderly sheep were dressed up to the nines, and perfumed, their fleeces carefully styled. The husband wore a neatly pressed white jacket and his wife a floral blouse. They were the last to enter the dining room, timidly, their arms linked.

'Let's move it, madam, let's move it, sir!' a waiter said to them.

There was nothing especially unkind about this, but Jefferson didn't like his familiarity. He himself was finishing his breakfast at the next table.

'Do you think he'd have said the same thing to a human guest?'

'I don't know,' replied Gilbert, dunking his third croissant in his hot chocolate. 'You do ask yourself strange questions.'

'Yes, I do. I wonder, for example, whether the humans don't look down on us a little.'

In actual fact, his impression could be summed up in a few words: the humans treated them as inferiors. At best, like children, at worst, like simpletons. He found this extremely disagreeable. And there was also the thorny issue of meals. The hotel manager had mentioned it in his brief welcome speech on the evening of their arrival. He had even tried to inject a note of humour, 'And of course, we have made every effort to ensure that you won't find any nasty surprises on your plates! Ha, ha, ha! Personally, I wouldn't like to come across a piece of my cousin or my sister, so I presume you wouldn't either.'

No one had laughed, not even Walter Schmitt, and the conversation moved on to other things.

Luckily, other humans showed them great respect, like Roxanne for instance, the young woman who was to be their guide during their stay. She was a geography student, like Jefferson, and she was financing her studies thanks to this job. She spoke English, French and Spanish. She wore second-hand clothes, had dishevelled orange hair and a permanent smile. Gilbert found from day one that she explained things so well that it made him feel clever too! Jefferson hadn't missed the opportunity to retort that that was indeed some achievement.

That morning, just after the breakfast incident, the twenty-seven Globetrotters, together for better or worse, walked to Granville cathedral. They went down the narrow cobbled streets of the old town and, as they passed a haberdashery called *Simone's*, Walter Schmitt insisted on taking a photograph of the mournful rabbit whose name was Simone posing under the shop sign. He made her pose and smile. She weakly tried to refuse but couldn't stand up to the boar. The fat Angora cat, trussed up in his raincoat, always lagged behind, oblivious of the others and took snaps of almost everything – cars, advertising hoardings, newspaper kiosks.

It wasn't very warm in the cathedral square and Roxanne, attentive to everything, was careful to gather her little group in a patch of sunlight. She launched into a passionate explanation. 'I must tell you, ladies and gentlemen, that it was following the great plague of 1642 that a pilgrimage . . .'

'1642! Woah! That's a long time ago!' remarked Mr Schmitt.

His concentration span was no more than three minutes. Beyond that, he couldn't help commenting. 'Darling . . .' his wife scolded, but he was unstoppable.

Roxanne continued, '. . . a pilgrimage was

organised to thank the Virgin Mary for protecting the population . . .'

They all listened attentively, like well-behaved school children. Mr and Mrs Cousins, the two sheep, continuously nodded their heads in approval, while the two vixens were silent.

Roxanne finished her talk. 'And that, ladies and gentlemen, is how this magnificent edifice came to be built. Now, let's go inside. Kindly remove your hats, caps and other headgear . . . Look, I've taken mine off!'

So saying, she whisked off her beanie, freeing her flaming hair (which the two red squirrels might have envied). She waved her little *GLOBETROTTERS* flag above her head and marched towards the entrance. They all followed behind.

The cathedral visit was fascinating and they were bowled over by the beauty of the nave, the columns, the stained-glass windows, the majestic organ and all the wonders designed and created by the humans. But Jefferson hadn't forgotten why he and Gilbert had come. Their investigation hadn't got off the ground yet and anxiety was gnawing away at him.

It was in the middle of the afternoon that things suddenly hotted up. Their coach was driving along the canal bank. Roland went slowly to allow his passengers to admire the reflections of the colourful facades shimmering in the water. Roxanne picked up the mic every now and then to point out a famous monument or building, or recount an anecdote.

'This house on your left is called the Nun's House, because it was the home of a very young girl whose father wanted to marry her off to an old miser and . . .'

Suddenly, Gilbert almost leaped out of his seat. 'Jeff! It's here!'

There was no doubt about it. The pretty footbridge over the canal, the brightly painted houses, the trees, a few moored barges. Jefferson fished the postcard out from his inside jacket pocket. He'd carefully kept hold of it ever since Sophie had entrusted it to him. It was all there, even the cyclists! They had to stop themselves from shouting, 'Roland! Stop here! We're getting off!'

Jefferson restrained Gilbert by his sleeve. 'Leave it! We'll come back tonight.'

The footbridge was a long way behind them and Jefferson carried on gazing at the postcard, intrigued.

'What are you looking at?' asked Gilbert.

Jefferson hesitated for a moment, then said, 'Gilbert, what do you see there?'

He pointed the nail of his little finger at a detail on the photo, the front door of a house on the other side of the river. Gilbert screwed up his eyes.

'Nothing. I see nothing.'

'But yes! Look! There!'

'You mean that little black dot?'

'Yes. It looks as if it's been made with a felt-tip pen, doesn't it?'

'Maybe. So what?'

'Well, it's not in the photo itself, so that means someone, probably Mr Edgar, wanted to indicate something, you know, like when you draw a little arrow on a postcard and write *We are here!*'

Gilbert took the card, moistened his index finger and pressed it down hard over the dot. A microscopic black comma appeared.

'Yes, it's felt-tip all right. But it looks as if he already tried to rub it out and didn't quite manage it.'

'You're right,' Jefferson went on. 'It's like that crossed-out sentence. In both cases, he was trying to say or show something.'

'Bravo, Sherlock Holmes!' said Gilbert excitedly. 'You never cease to amaze me!'

*

The visit to the Shoe Museum seemed as if it would never end, especially since Clarissa the hen, who was obsessed with slipper-making techniques, asked at least thirty questions on the subject. Meanwhile, Mr Schmitt was fooling around. He kept grabbing a shoe, sniffing the inside and telling anyone who'd listen, 'Oh yes, it's been worn!'

Gilbert and Jefferson thought they'd go crazy with impatience and, once back at the hotel, they barely took the time to get changed before rushing to the canal, their hearts pounding at the thought that their investigation was starting there and then, finally.

The neighbourhood was quiet that late afternoon. They stood still in the middle of the footbridge, noting the dozens of padlocks attached to the railings by lovers. Gilbert took a close look at one of them.

'Look at that, it's incredible! Look, it says *Sophie and Jefferson, eternal love!*'

Jefferson gave him a shove and they crossed over to the other side. The house that Edgar had marked with his felt-tip was number 42. The brick walls were ochre-coloured, the windows narrow. Were it not for the two pots of geraniums on the windowsill, it might look as if no one lived there. They approached. There was a name on the little brass plate: *Madeleine Rollet.*

Gilbert pressed the bell several times but it wasn't working. At least, they couldn't hear it ringing.

He knocked but received no answer. Their enthusiasm was somewhat dampened.

They set off to explore the neighbourhood. If Mr Edgar was known locally, maybe they'd come across someone who'd met him. Jefferson had the photo he'd cut out of the newspaper with him. He showed it first of all to a man in his fifties who was walking down the street, his newspaper under his arm.

'Excuse me, sir, have you ever seen this man by any chance?'

The tall man had to bend over to talk to little Jefferson. He replied with an amused smile, 'Possibly, but he's a badger, and they all look alike.'

They wound up in a little retro bar, opposite a barge. With a bit of luck, Mr Edgar might have come there for a drink. They both fancied a Coca-Cola, but they reckoned they'd be taken more seriously if they ordered two half-pints of beer. When the waiter brought them, he couldn't help saying snidely, 'A cushion, gentlemen, so you can reach the table?'

Gilbert shrugged and tried to say in a deep voice, 'No cushion, thank you. Have you ever seen this person in your bar?'

The waiter took the photo from him and looked at it carefully, not even bothering to hide his laughter.

'Ha, ha, ha! No! Definitely not! Because if I'd seen that face, I wouldn't have forgotten it.'

They left, their legs a little wobbly and their minds hazy. The outlook, right now, was gloomy. They were going to spend a week visiting the Beetroot Museum and the Sewing Machine Museum, putting up with Walter Schmitt's dubious jokes, not to mention Simone's sadness, which was contagious. And what would happen next? Gilbert would be able to go home with the Globetrotters, but what about Jefferson? He'd be left with a choice between life imprisonment back home or exile among the humans, alone for ever, a foreigner, lost. He felt a lump in his throat.

They stopped again halfway across the footbridge to watch a barge passing beneath them, but also to put off leaving. This place was their only chance of finding some trace of Mr Edgar, and leaving it meant they were defeated. They stared after the barge until it had disappeared around the first bend in the canal then, without consulting each other, their gaze fell on a little lady walking on the pavement down below, alongside the houses. She was carrying a heavy string shopping bag and had to change hands every four or five yards. They fell silent, but both secretly made the same bet, and when she stopped outside number 42 and fumbled in her pocket, they elbowed each other.

'Brill-iantl!' breathed Gilbert, clenching his fists.

They waited a little before knocking. They had to take care not to rush the elderly lady, or frighten her.

'Gentlemen?' she said, opening the door a chink.

She was taller than them, but very short for a human, and she could easily have been in her eighties, which put paid to the theory of a love affair, even if strange things do sometimes happen. She'd already taken off her jacket and put on a pinafore. A huge black-and-white cat was rubbing itself against her legs.

'Good evening, Mrs Rollet,' began Gilbert, politer than a vacuum-cleaner salesman and trying his best not to alarm her. 'We are friends of this person, do you happen to know him?'

She put on the glasses hanging from a chain around her neck.

'Oh, but that's Mr Charles!' she burst out at once, her mouth curving into a pretty smile. She looked up and it was as if the affection she bore Mr Charles spread to them too.

'Yes,' stammered Gilbert, without correcting her, 'it's Mr Charles. Do you know him?'

She laughed. Did she know Mr Charles! They were asking her whether she knew Mr Charles!

'Do come in, gentlemen, please.'

Her home was cramped and old-fashioned, but clean. The shopping bag full of provisions sat on a chair. The old lady invited them to sit at the kitchen table then brought them two glasses of blackcurrant cordial and a plate of shortbread biscuits. She put a saucepan of coffee to heat up on the gas hob for herself and poured a good half pint into a huge bowl decorated with a picture of Westminster Abbey. The cat had leaped up into Gilbert's lap and was shamelessly trying to woo him, contorting itself to find a comfortable position and purring in anticipation of being stroked.

'It's a she,' said Mrs Rollet. 'Her name's Josephine. She's very affectionate.'

'So I see,' grunted Gilbert.

'Go on, scratch her tummy. Scratch!'

'I'm scratching,' replied Gilbert, and sneezed.

They were both unaccustomed to household pets but they knew how much humans loved them, and it was important not to offend Mrs Rollet.

'Why didn't Mr Charles come last Sunday?' she asked.

'Something unexpected must have cropped up,' replied Jefferson.

He pictured the two cream-coloured shoes on the floor of Cut 'n' Dye, the scissors, the bloodstained overalls. He wasn't really being untruthful: something unexpected *had* prevented Mr Charles from coming.

'His business, probably,' added Mrs Rollet. 'I understand. He always told me I shouldn't worry if one day he stopped coming. Because of his business, as I was saying. That's why he paid me the rent for his room in advance. Always.'

'The rent for his room?'

'Yes, he has his room here, upstairs. He only uses it one night a week. He's been coming for two years now. And he's such a nice man. So tell me, how is he?'

Gilbert buried his hand deeper in Josephine's thick fur and opened his mouth to reply, but no sound came out. On the other hand, his nose began to run and he sneezed three times in a row. Meanwhile Jefferson sat twiddling his glass, at a loss, which was rare for him. The elderly lady looked from one to the other and waited for an answer. Then Jefferson took his courage in both hands. He looked up at her and said very softly, 'He . . . he's not very well.'

7

The elderly shed few tears but that doesn't mean they grieve less. Mrs Rollet was hunched up in her chair sobbing endlessly, pressing her handkerchief to her face. 'Oh, poor Mr Charles,' she moaned, as Jefferson told her the full story. She was even more upset when he mentioned Sophie.

'He adored her. He used to show me photos of her. Oh, poor, poor Mr Charles!'

Through her sobs she told them that he used to give her shampoo samples, hair colour and conditioner, and that at Christmas he'd made her a present of a variable temperature hairdryer, which she offered to show them. Oh, if only the murderer could be arrested and locked up. She certainly wouldn't be visiting him in prison.

'That is precisely why – *atishoo!* – why we've come

here, Madeleine, to arrest him. Could – *atishoo!* – could we have a look at Mr Ed ... Mr Charles' room?' asked Gilbert.

Jefferson was surprised at this 'Madeleine' and his friend's sudden familiarity, but when he turned to him, this detail was soon overshadowed by something much more spectacular. Gilbert's face had swollen and was covered in a red rash. His eyes had almost disappeared under his puffy eyelids, and Jefferson wondered if he could still see. His nose was streaming and he was sneezing almost non-stop.

'I think you should stop stroking that animal,' murmured Jefferson. 'You must have an allergy to cat hair.'

Mr Charles' room was spartan, and the furniture was minimal: a single bed with hospital corners, a cheap wardrobe, a little desk with no papers on it, a chair and a washbasin. The four walls and even the ceiling were covered in wallpaper that had a pattern of glass tumblers with straws. The window overlooked the canal.

'May I see inside the wardrobe?' asked Jefferson.

He had taken things in hand because Gilbert was not in any state to make himself useful. He was too busy sneezing, wiping his nose on his sleeve and gently kicking away Josephine, who was totally besotted with him.

'If it's for the investigation . . . then go ahead,' sighed the elderly lady. But when Jefferson opened the door and she saw the abandoned raincoat on its hanger, she sobbed all the harder.

'Poor, poor Mr Charles!'

Jefferson rummaged through the pockets but found only a handkerchief and an empty glasses case. There was still the desk drawer. He tried to open it but it was locked.

'Would you have the key to this drawer, Mrs Rollet?'

'Oh no! I don't have it. Mr Charles keeps . . . or rather *kept* it.'

'Do you perhaps have a spare?'

'No, I don't. I have one for the room, but not the drawer.'

If Jefferson had been alone, he'd have had no qualms about forcing it open, so eager was he to find a clue that might give them a lead, no matter how slender, but he couldn't do so in front of the landlady. He tried to question her about Mr Charles' activities, but sadly she knew nothing. He used to arrive on Sunday evening, have dinner with her, drink a herbal tea and go up to his room. That was their ritual. Then on Monday, he would disappear for the entire day, coming back in the late afternoon to pick up his bag, and take the night train home. He never discussed his business affairs. So what did they talk about? Idle chit-chat, this and that, she couldn't really say, but it was pleasant. Had anyone ever paid him a visit in his room? No, never. Perhaps she'd heard him telephoning someone? No, she didn't eavesdrop!

They thanked her and promised to come back later in the week. They found it hard to leave her alone with her grief, but there was nothing more for them to do there and they had to get back to the other Globetrotters at the Majestic Hotel.

As they walked through Granville, they were anything but unobtrusive.

'Why are people staring at me?' asked Gilbert in surprise when everyone they walked past turned around to look at him. 'Have I got toothpaste on my cheek, is that it?'

'It's a bit more serious than that, piglet. Take a look at yourself in that shop window.'

At first, Gilbert didn't recognise himself, then he leaped back, horrified.

'Is that me?

His face was even more swollen and the rash was worse. It made him look like an unknown variety of giant strawberry. Most people in his shoes would have begun to cry, but that wasn't Gilbert's style. On the contrary, he and Jefferson continued their walk across town, doubling up with laughter each time they glimpsed his grotesque reflection.

It was dinnertime at the Majestic, but Gilbert refused to show himself to the others in that state. They ordered two sandwiches and went straight up to their room, number 108, on the first floor. Roland, having been informed, at first laughed with them, then called a doctor who gave Gilbert an injection in his left buttock.

One hour later, the Elephant Man was resting on his bed, the swelling a little reduced. He was completely calm, his *Highway Code* in his hand.

'Did you know, Jeff, that if you're driving at 55 miles an hour, your total stopping distance will be 419 feet? That's perception, reaction *and* braking distance combined. And if you're driving at 70, you have to allow . . .'

Jefferson was sprawled on his bed too, the bedside table between them, but he didn't give two hoots about braking distances. He was staring at the ceiling, lost in thought.

'Gilbert?'

'Yes.'

'Maybe we're barking up the wrong tree. Maybe Mr Edgar's murder has nothing to do with here.'

Gilbert let his *Highway Code* fall onto his stomach. After a long silence, he launched into the following speech: 'You may be right, dear Mr Sangalli, yes, truly, you probably *are* right, *except* that . . . one: an inoffensive and worthy badger is murdered in his hair salon, in the Animal Kingdom. Two: an hour after the crime, a young hedgehog is almost crushed to death by a car speeding towards the border with two humans onboard. Three: we learn that Mr Edgar, that's the name of the victim, has been visiting the Land of the Humans every week for two years without saying a word about it to anyone, not even his nearest and dearest. Four: instead of staying at a hotel, which he could easily afford, he rents a room from a little lady under a false name, Mr Charles. Five: he sends a postcard to his niece on which he writes about humans: "*Sadly they can also . . .*" and crosses it out as if he's said too much. Where am I up to, six or seven?'

'Six,' said Jefferson.

'Then six: on that same postcard, he indicates his hiding place, with a microscopic dot made by a felt-tip, and it takes the eagle eye of the above-mentioned young hedgehog to spot it. Seven: he doesn't breathe a word of what he's up to here, not even to Mrs Rollet, his landlady. He simply talks about his "business affairs". Eight: in his room, he leaves no trace that could lead to him or to the people he deals with. There, Mr Sangalli, do you want me to go on? I don't know what you think, but *I* think that Mr Edgar, inoffensive hairdresser that he was, was involved in some dodgy business here, *risky* business, so risky even that it ended up costing him his life.'

Jefferson was flabbergasted.

'I say, is it your allergy that's stimulating your brain? I'm impressed. Rather than training to be a heating engineer, you should become an international lawyer.'

All the same, Gilbert's closing words had made a shiver run down his spine.

'Right,' he went on after a further silence, 'in short, we have to open that drawer, don't we? And I suppose you're not very keen on going back there.'

'You're absolutely right. Give Josephine my love and tell her I'm thinking of her.'

'Fine, I'll go on my own,' decided Jefferson, 'and

I'll open that drawer! What's the Globetrotters' programme for tomorrow morning?'

'I think we're hiring bikes to visit the park and the orangery.'

'OK, then I'll give it a miss.'

They switched off the light, but neither of them was able to sleep. At around midnight, Jefferson called out softly, 'Gilbert?'

'Yes?'

'Tell me. Supposing you've hidden something precious in a desk drawer. What do you do?'

'I lock it, of course.'

'OK. And what do you do with the key when you leave?'

'I put it in my pocket.'

'What if you don't want to keep it on you?'

'I hide it in the room.'

'Where?

'I don't know.'

'Me, I think I'd pull out the desk, bang a nail into the back, hang my key on it and push the desk back against the wall.'

When Gilbert woke up, he looked in the bathroom mirror and had a pleasant surprise: his face was back to its normal size and his eyelids were no longer puffy. Even though he was definitely a lot better, he was still spotty and caused a stir in the breakfast room where the two vixens, dermatology experts, offered him several creams which he refused. Jefferson wolfed down his breakfast, barely hearing Gilbert's encouragements, and hurried off.

He ran as far as the footbridge, happy to be acting on his own for once, and to have had, he hoped, a brainwave. A hundred times during the night he'd imagined slipping his hand between the back of the desk and the wall, a hundred times his fingers had come up against the nail, and a hundred times he'd yelled, 'Bingo!'

Mrs Rollet looked pleased to see him again so soon. She sat him down in the kitchen and, like the previous day, he had to drink a glass of blackcurrant cordial and eat some biscuits while she poured herself a large bowl of coffee. She must drink litres of it. Josephine was asleep, curled up on her blanket, oblivious.

'Is your friend better?'

'A lot better, thank you. The doctor came and gave him an injection. Everything's fine. Do you know what? During the night I thought—'

'You know, I barely slept,' interrupted Mrs Rollet. 'I was thinking about all the good times I had with Mr Charles. I'm going to miss him. Oh yes, I'm going to miss him—'

'I understand, Mrs Rollet. Anyway, I said to myself, in the night, that perhaps . . .'

'One Sunday evening, I'd made him a cheese soufflé and you know a soufflé has to be eaten straight away. I look at the clock: eight o'clock and no Mr Charles, a quarter past, and still no Mr Charles, and my soufflé's beginning to collapse! You can imagine my impatience . . .'

And mine! thought Jefferson, seething, and he stood up to cut her short. But he had to listen to the story of the soufflé to the end.

'As a matter of fact,' the old lady suddenly burst out, standing up and thrusting her hand in her pinafore pocket, 'last night I said to myself that maybe Mr Charles had hidden the key to the drawer in his room. I thought for a moment: where would I have hidden it if I'd had to? And then I had a brainwave. So I got up and went into his room. I ran my hand between the desk and the wall, and do you know what? It was there, the key! Hanging on a nail. Clever, eh? Are you still interested in it?'

They went upstairs together. The sun was filtering in through the curtains, bathing the room in a golden light. A barge went past on the canal. It was hard to imagine a more peaceful scene.

Jefferson turned the little brass key in the lock. The drawer was empty. All the same, he pulled it right out, took it from its housing, and turned it over. Then he slid his hand inside and explored the sides and the top, until his fingers encountered a slight bump. It was a piece of paper a couple of inches long, folded in two and Sellotaped to the wood. He eased it off and unfolded it. There were ten handwritten numbers, the first a 0 and the second a 7. It looked like a mobile phone number. Nothing more. But maybe that was already a lot. In any case, the number was important enough for Mr Edgar to have taken the precaution of hiding it carefully. That also meant he hadn't written it down anywhere else, probably because it was dangerous to keep it on his person.

As he put the scrap of paper away in his wallet, Jefferson had the feeling that Mr Edgar was beside him, like a timid little ghost. He wasn't wearing his hairdresser's overalls, but his coat.

He simply stood there and gazed at the young hedgehog with sadness. His eyes seemed to be saying:

Will that little scrap of paper be enough? and also: *Be careful. This is dangerous, you know . . .*

Jefferson slid his wallet into his pocket. 'Don't worry, Mr Edgar, Gilbert and I won't desert you.' He felt entrusted with a mission, and that inspired him with both pride and fear.

The fine weather had held, and Jefferson smiled as he pictured the motley group of Globetrotters cycling through the park. There was still time for him to join them, but he preferred to wander through the streets for a while. Was that the meaning of 'enjoying one's own company'? In any case, he was more acutely aware than ever that some humans looked at him with amusement, or even laughed at him. The children especially stared openly. He was the same height as them and they must have liked his hedgehog face.

One even asked out loud, 'Is that boy wearing a mask?'

And his mother, embarrassed, dragged him away.

Jefferson also walked past several people who had their dogs on a lead. This made him feel uncomfortable and he avoided looking at them.

8

The Globetrotters' afternoon was spent visiting a macaron factory about twelve miles away. Roland drove them there in his coach. They'd had to hoist Mrs Schmitt onto the coach, because she'd fallen off her bicycle in the park riding over a hosepipe. She had a huge bandage around her right knee and was in a great deal of pain, but she flatly refused to stay behind on her own at the hotel. It took four of them to get her onto the coach, directed by Walter, who proved to be a lot more concerned for his wife than they'd have thought. 'Are you all right, darling?' he asked her every second, and he kept a close watch on her, fussing and fretting, and urging: 'Gently, boys, gently . . .'

At the macaron factory, they were allowed to make the famous little meringues themselves. They all put on aprons and followed the pastry chef's instructions. There's nothing like a shared activity to help a group bond, and everyone was in a cheerful mood as they made the creamy filling, mixed the ingredients and wielded the piping bag. The two vixens confessed they never cooked at home and said what fun this was. The cat, curiously, was a bit behind all the time, looking more nonplussed than ever. Mrs Schmitt followed everything from her chair, probably hoping at least to be able to take part in the tasting at the end.

Jefferson, who loved making cakes, managed to forget about his investigation for a brief while. But soon enough his thoughts returned to that telephone number tucked away in his wallet. Who was at the other end? Who would answer it? And what would he say to them?

Jefferson and Gilbert were putting their macarons in the oven when Clarissa the hen, the one who'd asked fourteen thousand questions about how slippers were made, slid between them. She seemed all excited.

'It's Mr and Mrs Pearl's silver wedding anniversary,' she whispered. 'I'm organising a little present for them. Will you make a contribution?'

'Who are they?' asked Gilbert idiotically.

'The two squirrels.'

She'd become friendly with the couple and thought it would be nice to give them a small gift to celebrate the occasion.

'Of course,' agreed the two friends, and they both slipped her some money.

At the end of the afternoon, they were allowed to take their macarons away with them in elegant little boxes, but they'd barely driven a few miles before the two vixens had already eaten all theirs and boasted about it to anyone who'd listen. They were both skeleton-thin and could eat anything without putting on a single ounce, which exasperated Mrs Schmitt and a few other podgy ladies.

The road followed a river and Roxanne, mic in hand, told them about the tides, the locks and the sawmills. They then drove through a less attractive industrial zone. As usual, the cat, who hadn't left his seat at the back since the start of the trip, photographed everything. Roxanne sat down again. They drove in silence for a while because for once, Roland had been considerate enough not to put on the radio.

'What's that thing?' asked Walter Schmitt suddenly,

pointing to an elongated building with grey walls on the riverbank to their left. Two trucks covered with wire mesh were parked in front of it.

'Oh, nothing of interest . . .' replied Roxanne. But everyone could tell she was uncomfortable.

'Meaning what?' insisted Walter Schmitt. He wasn't the sort to be satisfied with a half-answer.

'Well, that's . . . that's the municipal abattoir.'

All eyes turned towards the building and stared at it until it was out of sight. No one spoke. Roland turned on the radio.

After dinner the hen presented the squirrel couple with their gift. She had chosen a stoneware water jug with a hideous decoration, it has to be said, but the elderly lovebirds were so overcome with emotion that it was contagious. Everyone sang *Happy Anniversary*. The two squirrels cried and said they hoped everyone would experience a love like theirs, embraced, and then went around the room kissing all the Globetrotters, including those who hadn't given anything. Jefferson, who was tender-hearted, was on the verge of tears himself.

'When you think about it, this package tour isn't so naff after all,' he said to Gilbert.

He was surprised to receive a gift from Simone. She came up to him shyly and gave him a packet of pills.

'Here, this is for you. Because you didn't show up this morning, I asked your friend and he told me you were tired. I'm sure it's your liver. So here's some black radish. Take one tablet every morning for a month and you'll feel better.'

They didn't go up to their rooms until about half-past nine as dinner went on longer because of the anniversary. Jefferson sat on the edge of his bed, opened his wallet, took out the scrap of folded paper and passed it to Gilbert.

'Here, my friend. This is what we've achieved after three days' investigation: a telephone number.'

Gilbert sat down next to him, looking pensive.

'I really wonder what Mr Edgar was up to here. Do you have the slightest idea?'

'Not the faintest,' replied Jefferson, and that was the honest truth.

They had ruled out a love affair. No, Mr Edgar didn't have a secret life. They'd wondered about political involvement, but the good hairdresser wasn't an activist, or if he was, he'd kept it very secret. Financial, then? Not that either. Nothing in his behaviour revealed a taste for money. He lived on little, and seemed to be very content with what he had. They'd thought about drug trafficking, but the idea of 'Mr Edgar' in connection with 'drug trafficking' simply made them howl with laughter. It was hard to imagine the quiet hairdresser from Cut 'n' Dye doing deals with drug barons between two perms. All they had were those ten numbers scribbled on a scrap of paper and the total mystery they concealed.

'You can't use your own phone,' Gilbert reminded him. 'Otherwise they'll be able to locate you. So you must use mine to call.'

'Why me?' retorted Jefferson.

'Well because it concerns you somewhat. Let me remind you that I'm not the one who's accused of anything, and that right now I should be learning how to install a room thermostat, not making macarons.'

Jefferson had to face the facts: it was up to him to act. Except that there were a lot of questions. The first was how he should introduce himself to the person who answered. Above all, how to make sure they didn't cut him off immediately, because if they did, the slender hope of learning something about Mr Edgar's killers would be dashed.

Gilbert went to brush his teeth and Jefferson did too, trying to gain a little time. Then they sat on the bed again and tried to come up with a strategy. Gilbert suggested practising by role playing. Jefferson would be himself and he would act the person on the other end. In theory, it was a very good idea, but at the first attempt, Gilbert couldn't help fooling around. He replied, 'Yes, this is Mrs Kristiansen, how can I help you?' in the bleating voice of the nanny goat, after which he spent a quarter of an hour writhing on the carpet with laughter.

It was nearly ten o'clock when Jefferson finally felt ready to call.

'Don't you think it's a bit late?'

'No!' said Gilbert, impatiently. 'Put it on speakerphone and do it! Now!'

Jefferson slowly keyed in the ten numbers, his stomach in a knot. The ringing sounded very far away and faint. They waited for the eighth ring and Jefferson was about to stop the call, more relieved than disappointed, when a woman's voice could be heard, 'Yes?'

Jefferson recited his speech. 'Good evening, madam. My name's Jefferson and I'm a friend of Mr Edgar's. He gave me your number and—'

'I don't know any Mr Edgar. I'm sorry. Goodbye.'

'Wait! It's Mr Charles, in fact. Mr Charles, do you know—'

'I don't know any Mr Charles either. Goodbye.'

The phone went dead.

'There we are,' said Gilbert.

'There we are,' said Jefferson.

The worst-case scenario had just happened. They were back to square one and even worse, now they'd lost hope.

'Maybe I should have gone about it differently . . .' Jefferson began.

'No, no, it's not your fault,' Gilbert consoled him. 'You were perfect. She didn't give you a chance. How about heading down to the bar for a drink. There's no point going to bed, we'll never be able to sleep after all that.'

The idea of having a drink at the hotel bar gave Jefferson the impression he was in a detective novel, except he didn't feel up to it. Would he have to drink a whisky, the disgusting stuff that tasted like medicine?

They were just leaving when Gilbert's phone, which he'd left on the bedside table, began to vibrate and jiggle around. Jefferson raced over to it.

'Yes?'

'Hello. It's me, calling you back. Apologies for earlier, I put the phone down on you.'

'No, no, please . . .'

'I'd like to ask you a question before going any further. For security. Don't be offended.'

'Not at all. Go ahead.'

Gilbert had also rushed over and was gesticulating frantically, *Put it on speakerphone! On speakerphone!*

'Right,' went on the amplified voice. 'Mr Edgar had a niece. What's her name, please?'

'Sophie,' replied Jefferson with the speed of a TV game-show contestant. 'Yes, Sophie.'

He had been alert enough to notice the past tense she used to speak about Mr Edgar: he *had* a niece. Which implied that the woman knew about his death.

'Good,' she went on, her voice softer, 'you really are a friend of Mr Edgar's. We can talk. Who are you, in fact?'

And who are you? Jefferson wanted to reply, but he was afraid of jeopardising the good relations they'd just begun. It's always difficult to say in a few words who one is.

'Well, I'm . . .'

Gilbert, next to him, began to jump up and down.

To help him, he pointed to his snout, pulling a face, and indicated Jefferson's nose and pointy ears.

'Oh yes, of course,' Jefferson said. 'I'm a hedgehog. I come from the Animal Kingdom. And my friend is a pig, because yes, we came together and we—'

'You mean you're here, in town?'

'Yes, we're at the Majestic Hotel. We'd like to talk to you.'

The voice paused. 'Are you on a package tour?'

'Yes, that's right.'

A silence, and then, 'Is there, by any chance, a boar in the group who's rather . . .'

'. . . annoying?' Jefferson helped her, since she couldn't find the word. 'Yes, that's right. Do you know us?'

'It's possible. And what do you want us to talk about?'

'Well, about Mr Edgar, and what happened to him . . .'

There was a fresh silence.

'OK. Do you know The Blue Note?'

'The . . . ?'

'The Blue Note, it's a jazz bar in the old town. Just ask, everyone knows it. In half an hour, does that suit you?'

Gilbert nodded his head vigorously and was already getting his jacket.

'Perfect. We'll be there. And um . . . how will we recognise you?'

'Don't worry, I'll recognise you. Oh yes, by the way, how did you get my telephone number?'

Jefferson decided to put his cards on the table.

'We found it in Mr Edgar's room at Mrs Rollet's . . . It's a bit complicated . . .'

'Fine, you can tell me all about it at the bar. See you later.'

9

As he walked through the narrow, ill-lit streets of the old town to The Blue Note, Jefferson no longer felt as if he was in a detective novel but in a film. When he caught the reflection of his puny hedgehog shape in a shop window, he couldn't help wondering whether the film company hadn't made a serious casting error.

'Do you think they'll let us in?' he fretted.

'Yes, it's a Tuesday. It'll probably be a quiet night. If it was Saturday there wouldn't even be any point trying.'

Gilbert was right, they had no difficulty getting in and they climbed the rickety stairs up to the first floor. There was nothing particularly jazzy about The Blue Note except the piano, which a tall guy in a hat was idly playing, and a few old posters of African American musicians on the walls. In truth, the atmosphere was a bit sad. A dozen or so people were slumped in the chairs or sitting on stools at the bar.

They ventured inside, a little intimidated. Neither of them were used to this type of establishment, and, most importantly, there were only humans there. The bartender welcomed them with a friendly, 'Good evening' and gestured to them to sit down at a table. They were about to do so when a youthful voice from behind them said, 'I'm the person you're looking for, I think, gentlemen?'

They turned around and their jaws dropped. The young woman was sitting in a dimly lit alcove, but her shock of orange hair left no doubt: Roxanne! She laughed at their stunned faces.

'Surprise! You see, I recognised you! Not hard.'

They'd barely sat down when the waiter arrived. He wiped the low table and lit a candle. 'Madam? Gentlemen?'

'I'll have a whisky,' said Roxanne.

Gilbert asked for a whisky too.

'Cocoa, please,' said Jefferson.

They sat in silence until the waiter was out of earshot. The situation was unexpected to say the least.

'What a coincidence!' began Roxanne. 'I'm curious to hear how you knew Mr Edgar. Were you friends of his?'

'Oh,' replied Jefferson, 'we weren't exactly friends. I was his customer, as a matter of fact. He'd been doing my hair for years. And Gilbert went there too on occasion, didn't you Gilbert?'

Gilbert agreed.

'You've heard what happened to him?' Roxanne went on.

They both nodded sadly.

'And do you know why they did that to him?'

They shook their heads. It was an awkward conversation between strangers, and they weren't sure how to begin. A sort of verbal tiptoeing around each other.

'What about you?' enquired Gilbert. 'How did you know Mr Edgar? Are you . . . in hairdressing?'

'Do I look as if I am?' asked Roxanne, pointing to her tousled mop, and she burst out laughing. 'Let's say we were fighting for the same cause.'

They waited but she didn't seem inclined to say

any more for the time being. The waiter brought their drinks. She waited for him to go away before continuing, 'I like your group. I think there's a very nice atmosphere. It's not always like that.'

'And we like you too!' was Gilbert's heartfelt reply. 'We all do!'

With that, they raised their glasses. Jefferson clinked his mug against the two glasses of whisky and then suggested getting down to the subject that really mattered. He decided to speak first, starting at the beginning, otherwise they'd never get anywhere.

'So, last week, I wanted to go and get a haircut at Cut 'n' Dye.'

'You wanted to go and *have your quiff trimmed*,' broke in Gilbert, smiling.

'Yes, whatever. I set off on foot and, on the road, I was nearly run over by . . .'

He told Roxanne the whole story: the car with the two humans, the scissors planted in Mr Edgar's chest, his running away, their visit to Sophie, the postcard, the package tour, old Mrs Rollet, the telephone number . . .

Roxanne listened attentively and, when he'd finished, she opened her handbag and took out a photo which she put down on the table. They didn't

need to look closely to recognise Mr Edgar's body, lying on the floor of his hair salon. It gave Jefferson a jolt.

'But who took that photo? The scissors are still in the wound, and it was me who took them out.'

'The people who killed him took the photo,' she said. 'And it is probably the same people who put copies in all our letterboxes. To scare us. Or rather to terrorise us. And the worst thing is, they've almost succeeded.'

'Your letterboxes ... *whose* letterboxes?' asked Gilbert clumsily.

This was it. They were finally going to understand.

'You don't know anything about Mr Edgar's activities in the human world? Really?'

They shook their heads.

'No, nothing.'

She took a sip of whisky and allowed a few seconds to go by.

'For the past few years, Mr Edgar had been an activist fighting industrial meat-farming, animal transportation and slaughter. Like me. There are several hundred of us. We secretly film inside the slaughterhouses so that people will know what really goes on within those walls. It's forbidden and it's dangerous. That's why we take all these precautions. I was the one who found him lodgings with Mrs Rollet. As far as she's concerned, he was Mr Charles. He frequently changed his name.

Jefferson had heard of the gruesome films that young people managed to make inside the slaughterhouses, at great risk to themselves, to inform people of the horrific practices.

'But Mr Edgar would have been too old to climb over the walls, film and flee in the event of . . .'

'Of course. He never did that.'

'So what did he do, then?'

'Mr Edgar was the head of the nationwide network, in other words, some eight hundred people. He was in charge, he organised and made the decisions. He came here every week to meet the volunteers and to encourage and advise them. His database was back there, in your kingdom, as a security measure, but he insisted on seeing us regularly, *face to face*. He was our leader but he was a lot more than that. I'd say he was a bit like our grandfather.'

She paused and had another sip.

'And, um . . . you know the two guys who almost ran Jefferson over?' asked Gilbert. 'They could be Mr Edgar's killers.'

'Oh yes,' she said. 'I know them only too well. They are two hit-men, in other words, two murderers. The tall, thin one is called Mackie, and the burly one, Red. Their combined IQs equal that of a shoe brush.'

'But what did they have against Mr Edgar?'

'Them? Nothing at all. They didn't give two hoots about Mr Edgar. For them, he was just a contract to be executed, so to speak.'

'A contract?'

'Yes, an order from the Abattoirs Association, I presume, or it could even have come from higher up in the meat industry. Hard to know. It's not the kind of information you read in the newspapers . . .'

She was still holding the photo of Mr Edgar. She slipped it sadly into her bag.

'I was very fond of him. He'd tease me about my hair, because I change styles every couple of months and I play around with colours. He always used to say that his great dream was for me to go and visit him, in your kingdom, and to turn up unannounced at his salon and ask him to do my hair as he liked. I'd probably have come out looking like my mother, but it would have been fun. I'd have done it. I *was* going to do it.'

She stopped talking. Her eyes had misted over. Jefferson recalled the kind, gentle badger of Cut 'n' Dye. *Hello, Mr Jefferson. Have a seat. Sophie will shampoo you. What will it be for you today? Just the quiff or the full spring haircut?*

A lump came to his throat. He pushed away his cup of cocoa and reached for Gilbert's glass. 'Can I have a swig of your whisky, please?'

10

In the lobby of the Majestic Hotel, there was a newspaper stand for the use of guests and the animals were pleasantly surprised to find *The Daily Trumpet* on it when they went down to breakfast. It was bound to be the previous day's edition, but they pounced on it, anxious to have news from home. The Cut 'n' Dye affair was still on the front page. Mrs Hild, the badger, was the keenest and, given the nature of the item, the others readily allowed her the privilege of being the first to read it.

'Listen,' she said in a voice quavering with emotion.

'Although we must presume innocence, there can be no doubt that JPS, hedgehog, is guilty. Many think his escape is highly suspicious. As for Mrs Kristiansen,

*goat and chief witness to the murder, she is completely
sure about her initial statements and has repeatedly
confirmed them (see below). The funeral of Mr Edgar,
badger, will take place tomorrow, and there is no
doubt, given . . .'*

Saying Mr Edgar's name made her choke up and
she was unable to read on. Her husband took over:

*'. . . there is no doubt, given how highly respected he
was in our town, that there will be a huge turnout.'*

Then he went on to the text in the box and to
Mrs Kristiansen, whose daily testimonies had become
a real saga.

*'I wanted to run away, but he was blocking my path
to the door, brandishing the bloodstained scissors. He
yelled that it was my turn, he called me an "old goat"
and "old nag" and he rushed at me. We rolled on
the floor. We fought hand to hand. I bit him. I saw
him close up, he had the devil in his eyes. I don't
know how I managed to get away from him.'*

Clarissa the hen, who was standing next to Jefferson

whispered, 'It must feel weird knowing that the murderer is . . . a hedgehog, I mean . . . someone like you.'

He shrugged and made an apologetic face, but was careful not to open his mouth, first of all because he had no comment to make but above all because he'd just taken one of the black radish capsules given to him by Simone and, according to Gilbert, it made his breath smell as if he'd just eaten his own socks.

The conversation at The Blue Note had gone on late into the night. At around one o'clock in the morning, Hugo, Roxanne's boyfriend, had joined them and they'd reminisced at length about Mr Edgar. Hugo had explained that in their opinion, he'd been killed at home, in the Animal Kingdom, because those who'd ordered the murder didn't care about investigations carried out over there, whereas here in Granville it was riskier for them, even if the victim was a badger.

Then they'd explained how they went about secretly filming in the abattoirs. Hugo had made a few videos, the first one by getting a job there for six months, the others by slipping unseen into the buildings. Roxanne had made a few too.

'Your heart's pounding,' she told them. 'You know it's prohibited, illegal, but you also know that it's for a good cause, that it's morally right, that you have to do it. For some months, Mr Edgar and we were planning a spectacular operation. We were going to make about thirty videos and release them all at the same time to create an internet sensation. The whole thing was scheduled for next year. But there was a leak, apparently. And look what happened . . .'

Jefferson had listened to the two young people and felt very small compared with their bravery. He had also felt slightly guilty. After all, as animals, they were the ones who should have been leading the struggle, whereas they were leaving it all up to the humans.

'Yes,' he grumbled as they made their way back to the hotel through deserted streets, at two o'clock in the morning. 'It's as if there are several categories of living beings, you see, with a clear hierarchy. At the very top, the humans, who take great pride in their superiority. Below them, there's us, who the humans look down on, but we can talk and are able to stand up for ourselves a little. Below us are pets, who can't talk, but who the humans have chosen. They give them names and protect them. And right at the bottom, there's the sub-category of farm animals, bred for their meat . . . and they, my friend, have a lot to fear!'

Furious, he kicked a metal dustbin, making a

loud clang in the silence of the night, and Gilbert had to restrain him.

'Stop it, Jeff, we'll get ourselves into trouble. That's crazy. One sip of whisky and you totally lose it! And don't forget we're here to find Mr Edgar's killers, not to change society!'

The Globetrotters had free time the entire following day. Even so, Roxanne put in an appearance at breakfast to say hello and advise them where to shop for souvenirs without getting too badly ripped off. She even offered to go with anyone who didn't feel confident.

Jefferson and Gilbert were leaving the hotel when they heard someone trotting behind them to catch them up.

'May I join you? If it bothers you, then say so, but as I'm all on my own . . . I'm anxious about being harassed in town . . .'

Simone, for it was she, barely waited for them to reassure her with a, 'Yes, of course, it'll be a pleasure'. She had already squeezed herself between them and grabbed their arms, and now she clung to them. The fact she was wearing hiking shoes and a backpack showed she intended to be wandering the city for hours.

'Oh, thank you so much! Where are you thinking of going shopping? I don't want to impose.'

'Actually, we don't have any definite plans and . . .' stammered Gilbert.

She was tall and thin, her two long, floppy ears falling onto her shoulders. Gilbert came up to her armpits and Jefferson to her hips. The trio would not go unnoticed in town.

'Well I'd like to find some little fridge magnets,' she said, 'and a vegetable grater. I live on my own, you see, and I often have raw vegetables.'

'Ah,' said Gilbert, 'it should be easy to find all that.'

Neither of them dared to tell her the truth. *You know, dear Simone, we are very fond of you, but right now we have very little interest in vegetable graters. As a matter of fact, we're on the trail of two murderers.*

She dragged them into several hardware stores, but the graters were never quite what she was looking for, and in the end they gave up. At around eleven o'clock, they set off in search of the fridge magnets and had more luck. She found one depicting the Granville skyline and bought it on the spot, then she insisted on buying one for each of them.

'This is for my valiant bodyguards,' she explained.

They were looking for a restaurant with a terrace where they could have lunch in the sun, when Jefferson stopped dead in the middle of the street and dived into a shoe shop.

'What's got into you?' asked Gilbert. 'Do you want to buy some trainers?'

Jefferson kept his hands by his sides but was jerking his chin frantically in the direction of the opposite pavement.

'Eeeeeeek! Yiiiiiiikes! Tharaghe taragoo haragumaragans! Tharaghe taragoo haragumaragans!' he mumbled.

'What are you saying?'

'The two humans! Over there!'

A quick glance and Gilbert spotted them too. Jefferson had described them in enough detail. The tall one with the shaven head was scraping away at a scratchcard at the counter of a newsagent's. He could be clearly seen through the window. The other, with his woollen beanie and his athletic body in a tight-fitting black T-shirt, was waiting for him outside, puffing away on a cigarette.

'Are you certain?'

Jefferson was shaking from head to foot.

'Yes, it's them.'

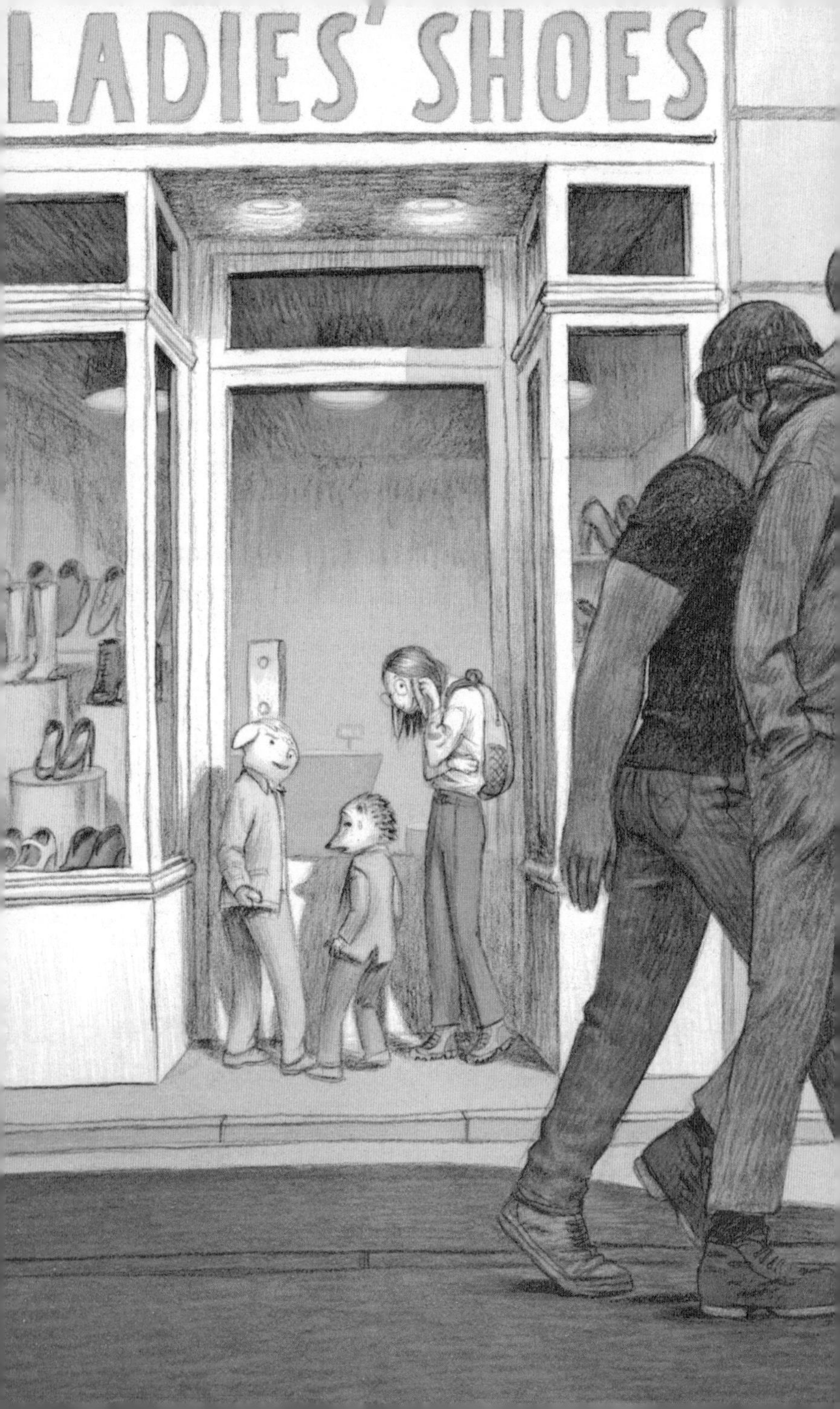
LADIES' SHOES

Simone, who had joined them, was surprised to see one of her bodyguards in such a state.

'Oh, my goodness, what's wrong with him?'

'It's nothing,' Gilbert reassured her. 'He's just seen two old friends he'd lost touch with ages ago and it gave him a shock.'

'So I can see,' she said. 'He's so sensitive. I like that in a man, you know. Sensitivity.'

Jefferson grew more and more agitated. He looked as if he was about to pass out.

'Gilbert, look! They're leaving!'

The tall, thin one had come out of the shop, without having won anything judging from his scowl, and the pair were already striding off.

'We've got them, hedgehog!' whispered Gilbert. 'Stay with Simone. I'll follow them!'

Jefferson didn't have a chance to stop him. He heard Gilbert mutter 'Brill-iant', and saw him weave in and out of the passers-by in pursuit of the two killers.

'Take care!' he shouted after him, suddenly feeling convinced he should never have let him go.

Lunch with Simone in these circumstances felt really bizarre. He had the sense of being two people. Half of him tried to listen to the sad rabbit and make polite conversation, while the other half was alongside the unfortunate Gilbert who'd probably already been caught by two thugs twice his size and three times his weight, two guys who had no qualms about stabbing an amiable hairdresser in the chest with a pair of scissors.

Simone, slightly tipsy from a glass of white wine, soon launched into the saga of her love life and her attempts to find a life partner which always ended in failure. The most recent one seemed to have got off to a good start, however. She'd corresponded for a long time with a young buck-rabbit and they really seemed to click. They'd exchanged photos. And then, on the day of their first real date, he'd quite simply stood her up . . .

'So, he hopped it,' commented Jefferson, whose thoughts were elsewhere.

'Sorry?'

'No, nothing. I'm sorry. I meant that was despicable of him.'

'Last year, I also met a double bass teacher . . .' she began.

'. . . who was perhaps more attuned to you?' ventured Jefferson, not very proud of himself.

'And what about you?' she asked all of a sudden. 'Do you live alone? Am I being too nosy, or stupid? Maybe you're . . . I mean . . . you and Gilbert—'

'No,' interrupted Jefferson, 'we're just friends.' He really couldn't stand any more. 'Why don't we go back to the hotel?' he suggested. 'I'm feeling a bit tired, to be honest.'

'Your liver!' she exclaimed. 'Did you take your capsule this morning?'

They carried on walking for part of the afternoon, running into the cat, who was photographing a flower bed in a little park, and the elderly sheep couple who Roxanne was helping to buy a tartan rug in a souvenir shop. Jefferson had to stop and chat with them, give his opinion on the colour, and lie about Gilbert's absence. His phone in his pocket remained worryingly silent.

The minute he was back in his room, he rang Roxanne. Too bad if he risked giving himself away. She answered straight away and he could hear from the tone of her voice how delighted she was to talk to him.

'Oh, Jefferson! Is everything all right? You looked worried earlier. Has something happened?'

'Yes, Roxanne, something has happened . . .'

She thought the best thing was to wait patiently for Gilbert to give some sign of life. In any case, there was no need to panic. She comforted him as best she could and left him with the promise that she'd call back that evening. Despite these reassurances, Jefferson lay on his bed brooding, unable to read or to watch television. On Gilbert's bedside table sat the *Highway Code* and *Alone on the River*, with a bookmark at page four. The afternoon dragged on endlessly.

Dinner was an opportunity for the Globetrotters to tell each other about their day's purchases. 'What did you find?' they asked one another and they showed off their trophies. Jefferson, gloomy, was sitting with the two squirrels and Clarissa the hen, and was thinking, *Well I didn't find anything. On the contrary, I lost everything. I'm useless.* And when Roland came and asked him where his cousin was, he almost began to cry. He checked himself in time and explained that Gilbert had bumped into some friends and was spending the evening with them and apologised for abandoning the group for one evening.

While they were having dessert, one of those little things happened that perk you up when you're down. Often it's a very little thing, but it cheers you up. Mr and Mrs Hild, the two badgers, who hadn't spoken a word to him since the start of the trip, came timidly over to him and asked if they could sit with him for a moment. They wished to talk to him.

'You see, Mr Sangalli,' began the husband, 'my wife and I had decided to ignore you because, to tell you the truth, we were very upset by the murder committed by that young hedgehog. In fact, it happens that we knew Mr Edgar well. So we didn't want to have anything to do with you. And then, with the passing days ...'

'... yes,' continued his wife, 'with the passing days, we said to ourselves that it was ridiculous and stupid. Because you're in no way to blame. So we'd like to apologise for our behaviour towards you and ask if you would shake hands with us.'

They had spoken so eloquently and movingly that Jefferson, who'd been on edge for several hours, felt the tears running down his cheeks. He held out both hands to take theirs and stammered, 'But of course ... it's ... I completely understand ... thank you. In any case ... thank you ... I'm very touched ...'

They were emotional too, and all three of them felt that strange, deep happiness that comes from reconciliation.

When Roxanne called, it was almost midnight and Jefferson had to disappoint her: there was no news of Gilbert. And that wasn't like him. Something was wrong. She suggested that maybe his phone battery was dead. That he would reappear a bit later, his usual cheerful self, and tell them everything. Jefferson mustn't fret.

Only Gilbert didn't come back, neither a bit later nor a lot later. He didn't come back at all and Jefferson spent the night dozing off and waking up with a start from a recurrent nightmare in which the car with the two humans in it was ceaselessly chasing him and running him over. He ended up being imprisoned in this car, at the bottom of a ravine, injured and unable to move. Someone was banging on the bodywork, outside, someone was trying to get in. He didn't know whether it was a friend come to help him or someone who wanted to harm him. They were knocking and banging, and banging some more.

Then, Jefferson woke up fully and realised that the noise wasn't coming from his dream but was very real. Someone was hammering on the door of room 108 of the Majestic Hotel, *their* room. The radio-alarm clock showed 6:45. He leaped up and grasped the door handle.

'Who is it?' he asked, instinctively suspicious.

'It's me!' answered Gilbert. 'Open the door!'

11

The creature who rushed in bore very little resemblance to the Gilbert that Jefferson had known since childhood. The poor thing was filthy, scratched, battered. His face, arms and hands were streaked with mud and blood, and his clothes were soiled. But the most striking thing was the wild look in his eyes.

'Where have you been?' squeaked Jefferson, aghast.

'To hell, my friend,' groaned Gilbert, and he rushed into the bathroom.

Jefferson heard the shower running for a long time.

'Are you OK?' he asked several times, but received no reply.

He used the time to leave a message on Roxanne's voicemail: 'Gilbert's back.'

Then the sound of water stopped and Gilbert

emerged wearing the hotel bathrobe and looking rough. In the corner of the room was an armchair which they'd never used except to heap their clothes on. He flopped into it. Jefferson pulled up the desk chair beside him.

'Tell me all about it.'

'Right, I'll start at the beginning. That's best, isn't it?'

'Good idea,' Jefferson encouraged him with a smile. 'Take your time. Do you want something to eat first?'

'To eat, no. But I'd love a coffee.'

Jefferson went down to the bar to fetch him one. When he came back up to the room, he found Gilbert crying softly in the armchair.

'Tell me all about it.'

Gilbert blew his nose, wiped his eyes and took a deep breath.

'So, I leave you with Simone and start tailing the two thugs. They walk super fast and I have to trot to keep up with them. We leave the old town and reach a wide avenue, and I say to myself I'm exposed, they'll see me. But no, they vanish inside a little apartment building. I wait for half an hour, an hour. Nothing. They must be eating. I want to text you to tell you I'm giving up and coming back, but I find my phone's out of battery. Just then, the tall, thin one comes out, alone. The other one appears at a window on the second floor and yells, "Catch! You forgot your lighter." Of course I'm careful to note which window. The tall guy crosses the road, gets into his car, a black saloon, and drives off. I don't think twice, I jump onto a bicycle I've spotted leaning against a wall, not chained up, and I race after him. I say to myself, *I'm only borrowing it, I'll bring it back.* I pedal like mad. We go over the canal bridge and then I start losing ground. I just see him turning in the direction we took the other day for the macarons. I slow down and carry on calmly along the country road till I get to the industrial zone. I arrive at the abattoir, you remember, and I have a hunch. I ride into the car park and bingo! – the saloon's there. Our boy is definitely in business with the abattoir.

'I should have turned back there and then, Jeff. I'd located the other guy's apartment, that's already good going. But I don't know what got into me, I dumped the bike in the undergrowth and continued on foot. I said to myself, *You want an adventure, well this is it!* I imagined myself like Roxanne and Hugo, you see, I pictured myself as a hero.'

Jefferson saw very well, but he would have been content just to think of it.

'So, I slip unnoticed into the building while they're busy manoeuvring a livestock trailer full of sheep into the yard. Half-way up the wall I see a big hook. I grab it, climb the wall and hide in a recess in the metal framework. You know, people never look up. If you want to hide, go high up. And that's when the nightmare begins. First, they unload those poor sheep who are bleating plaintively. I don't know where they've come from, but I assure you they didn't travel with Globetrotters. They're crammed together, thirsty and panic-stricken. They're thrown around any old how. There's one that's limping, it has at least one broken leg, but they don't care at all, they beat it to keep it moving. Another one escapes. A guy catches it, picks it up by the hind leg and throws it over the gate.

'The sheep has lost its bearings and goes off in the wrong direction, dragging itself along. The guy picks it up by the same leg and throws it over the gate again. You see that and you want to scream. There's bleating and yelling. You can't hear people speak. The sheep know they're going to die, and they have no way of defending themselves. They don't

have a chance. Just suffer and die. So there I am, huddled up in my nook in the eaves and I daren't move. I'm terrified. I say to myself, *If they see you, they'll do the same to you.*'

'Do you want another coffee, Gilbert?'

'No, but I'd love a piece of bread or something now. I haven't eaten a thing since yesterday morning.'

Jefferson went downstairs. Several Globetrotters were already seated in the breakfast room. He greeted them politely, hurriedly grabbed a handful of pastries and took them up to room 108.

'Here, my friend, one at a time.'

Gilbert didn't devour them. He started nibbling slowly at a chocolate croissant.

'There was a lull and then, an hour later, they bring in . . . pigs. Pressed so close together that they can't even lie down to have a rest. Some try to escape, trampling on the others. You can see they're all in shock. Their tongues are hanging out. Most look crazed, and they're biting one another. Their ears and tails are bleeding. You can't begin to imagine, Jeff. And that's when I say to myself that they're my brothers in a way, my less fortunate brothers, you see and . . .'

At that he began sobbing and his face was

screwed up in a grimace that Jefferson had never seen before, even though they'd known each other since childhood. Crumbs of chocolate croissant moist with saliva dropped onto his knees.

'I can't tell you everything,' he gurgled. 'It's too awful for words: electric shocks to drive them forward, beating them with sticks – on their backs, behind the head and on the snout – pigs staggering, howling in pain, and they suffer it, they suffer it with no way to defend themselves. It's unjust. It's . . . outrageous. And then, they force them between two barriers, like down a corridor, beating them all the time, and then they disappear from view. But you know very well where they're going, don't you? They're going to have their throats slit while they're still alive, stunned a little, one after the other, methodically. The only thing the humans care about is how to kill as many animals as possible in the shortest possible time.'

He wiped his mouth and nose on his sleeve and went on, 'The time probably passed quickly because, suddenly, everything stopped. They hosed away the blood and mess. They changed their clothes, switched off the lights, locked the doors and left. And me, I was still up there on my girder, in shock. My teeth were chattering. I climbed down and hoped to get out through a door they might have forgotten to lock or a window left half-open. Impossible. So then I went exploring. It's vast, this place. There were loads of animals penned up waiting. I visited them all: pigs, sheep, cows. There was an old horse, all alone. I stroked his forehead. After that, I spent a long time with the cows. At dawn, the place was silent. You could only hear their breathing. They all had a number tag in their ear. From time to time, one of them would moo. It reeked of anxiety, Jeff, I swear. Nothing but concrete, metal and anxiety. I wanted to say to them: *It'll be all right, ladies*, but I knew very well that wasn't true, that it wouldn't be all right at all. When it was light and the humans came back, it would be very bad for them. I could hardly say: *It's OK, it's nothing to worry about, they only took your calf from you at birth or just after, drank your milk, the milk that was for your calf, and now they're going to slaughter you and take your meat and your hide. Does that arrangement suit you? Oh yes, I was forgetting, they ate your calf too, but in exchange for all that, they did give you some nice grass to eat, didn't they?* At around six o'clock, the sky grew light. I heard a car engine followed by the grating of a metal door opening. Then I said goodbye to everyone. Or rather *adieu.* I sneaked out. I found my bicycle and rode into town. I put the bike back where I'd found it and here I am.'

Gilbert closed his eyes.

'Right, I think I'll go to bed and try and get some sleep. I'm no good for anything at the moment.'

Jefferson plumped his pillow and drew the curtain.

'I won't disturb you.'

Gilbert got into bed and curled up under the blanket, but he wasn't able to stem the tide of words.

'It's incredible though, isn't it?' he mumbled, his voice muffled. 'They can eat whatever they like – spaghetti with basil, potato gratin, four seasons pizzas, fruit tarts, potato omelettes, carrot cakes, red lentil soup with coconut milk, pancakes with lemon, apples, pears, apricots, fried mushrooms, tomato salads, croissants, tagliatelle with pesto, vanilla custard, strawberries, melon, rice, mashed potato, peas, pumpkin soup, hazelnut chocolate . . . and *that's* not enough for them. They don't think it's enough, so they kill animals to eat them! I don't understand . . .'

Jefferson now sat in the armchair, in the dark, and waited.

Gilbert had trouble getting to sleep. From time to time brief sobs escaped him like hiccups, and feeble groans. When he was completely quiet and his breathing calm, Jefferson rose noiselessly and stole out of the room, taking two croissants as he went past.

12

The Globetrotters clambered aboard the coach.

'Where is it we're going?' asked Jefferson, who'd completely lost track of the programme.

'We're going to visit Sawlish Castle,' Mrs Schmitt informed him. 'And then we're going to have a picnic in the gardens, like school kids! That'll be fun, won't it?'

She was still limping slightly but was able to walk, clinging to her husband's arm.

During the journey, the two vixens asked Roxanne if they could borrow the microphone and they treated everyone to a concert of golden oldies. They'd chosen well-known songs and rewritten them using the names of all the Globetrotters. It was a bit naff, to be honest, but it made everyone laugh.

Jefferson resigned himself and valiantly put up

with the day's ordeals: the tour of the castle with a nonstop whispered commentary by the insufferable Clarissa, the dreadful snores of Mr Schmitt, who'd fallen asleep on the lawn, Simone's sudden and inexplicable tears, the spectacular tumble of Mrs Cousins, the ewe, who tripped on the footboard as she was getting onto the coach . . . On the way back, Roxanne managed to seat herself next to him.

'Well?' she simply asked.

'He spent the night inside the abattoir. He came back completely wrecked.'

She forced a smile and nodded. Having experienced that often enough herself, she understood.

'Is he resting now?'

'Yes, he's asleep.'

'That's good. He'll get over it. And so will you. Everything will be fine, Jefferson.'

She'd murmured 'Jefferson' softly, like a shared secret, and it made him feel all emotional. It reminded him of Sophie. Was she still defending him, back home? Defending his innocence, against the whole world and despite all appearances?

When they reached the hotel, he was the first off the coach. He scooted past reception, raced up the back stairs and knocked on the door of room

108. The cheerful voice from inside reassured him: Gilbert was feeling better! He came and opened the door, smiling, and dived back onto his bed.

'Sorry, I'm deep in my *Highway Code*. What do you reckon: on a sixty-mile journey, how much time do you save if you drive at eighty miles an hour instead of seventy: a) twenty minutes b) fifteen minutes c) six minutes?

'I don't know,' replied Jefferson. 'I must say you've recovered quickly!'

'Yes, I slept until three o'clock in the afternoon! Right, the answer's six minutes! That's crazy, isn't it? It's not worth risking your life.'

'Gilbert?'

'Yes?'

'Supposing we go back home. I'll hand myself in to the police and explain everything. That's what I should have done from the start.'

Gilbert let the book fall onto his belly.

'Woah, little hedgehog, does it take so little for you to lose heart? No, no, we're not going home at all. We've had a lovely Globetrotters trip, the town is delightful and our investigation's progressing every day, what more do you want?'

Jefferson sat down on the edge of the bed.

'Listen. I've been thinking about it all day, while you were napping. We have no chance of arresting these two guys, or of doing away with them, and even less of bringing them back to our country. We were dreaming. It was madness. I wonder how we could have imagined for one moment that . . .'

'Hold on. I've been thinking too. And I came to the same conclusion as you: those two are out-and-out thugs and they're professionals. With just the two of us, we'll never manage to corner them.'

'You see.'

'Two of us no, but . . .

'But?'

'But with twenty-seven of us, yes.'

It took Jefferson a few seconds to grasp what Gilbert was saying, and his jaw dropped.

'Forgive me for saying this, Gilbert, but I think that this time you're off your rocker. You're completely nuts. It must be the night in the abattoir that's addled your brain.'

'Not at all! I pinpointed the apartment of the guy with the hat, the beefy one, who's called Red, when he threw down the lighter. We all turn up there together and jump on him. There are twenty-seven of us, let me remind you, twenty-seven!'

'Twenty-seven, yes, but twenty-seven what, for goodness sake?' said Jefferson angrily. 'Twenty-seven nothing-at-alls! A couple of sheep so old that the lady falls flat on her face getting onto the coach, a female rabbit who bursts into tears twice a day for no reason, a tomcat who's completely spaced out, a crazy boar, two squirrels who faint with fear when you clap your hands – it's hardly the rapid response squad, is it!'

'Now listen, Jeff. Let me sum up where we're at: one: you haven't been arrested; two: we've picked up Mr Edgar's trail; three: we're onto his killers. And you want to stop there! It's a bit like a runner who's ahead of all the others in a race who gives up just before he passes the finishing line. I read that in a novel, and it's a great image. But I don't want that to happen in real life!'

Jefferson had to admit to himself once again that Gilbert could be very persuasive. Perhaps he was right and they had to see this through. Except that idea sounded completely bonkers.

'We'd have to convince the entire group. No way!'

'We can try. Now this is how we could go about it . . .'

*

That evening, after dinner, Roxanne perched on a chair and asked for a minute's attention from the Globetrotters, who were on their dessert – chocolate mousse, the house speciality. The two elderly sheep had tied their napkins around their necks so they wouldn't drop chocolate down their fronts.

'I apologise for interrupting your dinner. In the basement, there's a small meeting room. I'd like you to be there in ten minutes please. I promise you we won't be long. Thank you.'

They all looked at one another. If this was about tomorrow's itinerary, she could tell them about it here. It didn't usually take long and she didn't make a song and dance about it. But, ten minutes later, they all gathered obediently in the basement room. Roxanne asked them to sit around the boardroom table and thanked them for coming, then she turned to the flipchart, picked up a marker pen and wrote on the big white sheet: "GOOD NIGHT!"

With that, she brushed her lips with her fingertips, blew them a collective kiss and left the room, laughing. They didn't see her Sellotaping to the other side of the door an A4 sheet, on which she'd written:

```
┌─────────────────────────────────┐
│                                 │
│        GLOBETROTTERS'           │
│       SCRABBLE EVENING.         │
│                                 │
│      PLEASE DO NOT DISTURB.     │
│                                 │
└─────────────────────────────────┘
```

At first they were all dumbstruck, then they all started to talk at once. What did this mean? Had Roxanne taken leave of her senses or what?

Jefferson, seated at the head of the table, cleared his throat.

'If you please, if you please . . . Thank you.'

It took him a while to get them to settle down.

'Ok, here goes. Actually it's Gilbert and me who wanted to call this meeting, not Roxanne. Because it so happens that we have a lot of things to tell you. Yes . . . really a lot . . . so many even that I don't know where to start.'

'Start at the beginning,' Gilbert advised. 'I'll pick up when it comes to the bits concerning me.'

The Globetrotters sat there with eyes as round as saucers.

'Yes,' continued Jefferson, 'you're going to be very surprised. It's about the Cut 'n' Dye case.'

A murmur ran through the assembled group. The two badgers pricked up their ears.

'That morning, I mean the morning of the murder, I went to the salon to have my hair cut. I found the door locked and I went round to the back of the building. I climbed in through the window and I was the one who found poor Mr Edgar. He was lying on the floor, the scissors planted in his chest. Mrs Kristiansen was asleep under her dryer . . .'

'Hold on, Mr Sangalli,' broke in Clarissa the hen. 'How come you say you saw her sleeping whereas she claims—'

'My name isn't Sangalli,' Jefferson interrupted her. 'I'm called Jefferson Ponsonby-Smythe.'

This admission should have been a bombshell, causing pandemonium, shrieking and fainting, but it had the opposite effect: a chill silence fell over the group.

If someone had dropped a pen cap on the floor it would probably have unleashed a total panic, but nothing of the sort happened, and Jefferson was able to continue, 'Don't worry, I haven't ever killed anyone and I have no intention of doing so. I ran away because Mrs Kristiansen woke up and saw me holding the scissors which I'd just pulled out of poor Mr Edgar's body. I didn't think, I followed my instinct, I just wanted to help him. But then I was overwhelmed, not surprisingly. That lady started shrieking, she ran out into the street and named me as the culprit. I was so frightened that I ran away thinking I'd explain and defend myself later, calmly. I just wanted to go home, you understand . . .'

He carefully told them what had happened next: Sophie's postcard, which he showed them and even passed around; the opportunity of the Globetrotters trip to slip across the border unnoticed; Mrs Rollet, the discovery of Mr Edgar's fight to protect animals – a fight that had cost him his life – and lastly the coincidence of running into his two killers in town. He omitted unnecessary details like their dressing up as girls and Gilbert's allergy to cat hairs. The audiences' expressions gradually changed as his story unfolded. From amazement to interest and then compassion, particularly as Jefferson's final words were to apologise to his travel companions if he'd been a bit distant with them until now. It was because of all his worries, but in the meantime, he'd got to know them and appreciate them better. Then he handed over to Gilbert.

'What I have to tell you isn't funny,' he began.

Jefferson was afraid his friend would be overcome

with emotion again and not manage to finish his story, but he was wrong. Gilbert was able to move his audience to tears without breaking down himself. When he described the suffering of the sheep, Mr and Mrs Cousins blew into their handkerchiefs. When he spoke of that of the pigs, Roland let out a heartfelt curse. And when it was about the cows and their wait, in the silence of the night, the lady cow and her two nieces lowered their heads.

'But why are you telling us all this?' eventually asked Mr Pearl, the timid squirrel. 'I mean, what do you want from us?'

This was it.

Jefferson took over from Gilbert and explained as best he could, repeating word-for-word some of the things Roxanne had said at The Blue Note. It wasn't a question of waving a magic wand to change the humans' habits. That would take time. The only solution was for them to stop eating meat, or to eat less of it. As long as they continued, there'd be money to be made in meat, and humans would carry on slaughtering animals without asking themselves the slightest question. And they'd carry on having people believe that the animals were overjoyed at the idea of sacrificing themselves for them – just look at the happy faces of the pigs drawn on the windows of butchers' shops. It would be a very long battle and it would probably take several decades more, a century perhaps, before people would ask how they dared do that *in the old days*.

They nearly all nodded approval.

'It's like slavery or torture,' said Mrs Schmitt. 'For centuries, people thought it was normal . . .'

Jefferson realised he hadn't answered Mr Pearl. He had to go back to what he'd said. They weren't going to change the world that quickly, but they could at least, for the time being, not allow Mr Edgar's killers to go unpunished. But, reporting them to the humans' police had no chance of achieving anything. The murder of a badger counted for nothing here, in the Land of the Humans. And in the Animal Kingdom, the case seemed to have been judged in advance: he, Jefferson, was the designated culprit, and had been from the very first. The only way to obtain justice for Mr Edgar and prove Jefferson's innocence, was to arrest the killers themselves and bring them back in the luggage compartment of the coach, then hand them over to the police supported by evidence. And that was it.

Roland leaped up.

'In my luggage compartment! But I'm not allowed to! . . . Mind you, it would be quite funny, wouldn't it? So long as they keep quiet . . . I don't see how we could make them do that.'

Then he laughed and brandished his clenched fist. 'Well, yes I can, but that's not allowed either!'

'Yes,' continued Jefferson, 'that's one of the many problems to be resolved. There are others. Gilbert has located the apartment of one of the two killers. It's on a nearby avenue. We'd have to take him by surprise at home. With a bit of luck, the other one will be there too. But I'd like to say first of all that I completely understand if some of you don't want to get involved. It's not your profession or mine. But our best chance of pulling it off is if there are twenty-seven of us, or twenty-eight with Roland.'

Gilbert nodded.

'Twenty-eight against one, or against two.'

There was a silence, no doubt while each of them imagined what that 'take him by surprise at home' actually meant.

Then Mr Hild, the badger, spoke up as eloquently as ever: 'If I have understood you correctly, you are suggesting that we storm the residence of these individuals together, thus prevailing in numbers over their probable strength, storming in without warning and neutralising them so as to hand them over to the authorities, thus rendering them in no fit state to inflict further harm?'

'Um . . . yes,' replied Gilbert, slightly dazed by this flowery language.

The two vixens, for whom Jefferson did not feel any special fondness, rose up as one.

'We're in! We'll come. Those scumbags must pay!'

'I'm coming too,' boomed Walter Schmitt. 'And the shi—'

'Darling!' scolded his wife, stopping him just in time from uttering an inappropriate swear word.

'Wait,' said Jefferson. 'I don't want you to decide so fast. Take some time to think it over. I suggest we break for fifteen minutes and then come back here.'

Instead of going up to their room, Jefferson and Gilbert paced up and down the car park, behind the hotel. The little yellow coach was neatly stationed by the wall. *AVID FOR ADVENTURE? JOIN THE GLOBETROTTERS!* read Jefferson, and he thought, *This is some adventure!*

'Right, we've already got the two vixens and the Schmitts,' gloated Gilbert. 'It's a good start.'

Jefferson was less optimistic.

'Yes. We can also count on Mr and Mrs Hild, the badgers, they've got a personal score to settle, but the others . . . can you see Simone going into battle? Or Mr and Mrs Pearl, the squirrels? Or Clarissa?'

'If half of them sign up, it's do-able,' reckoned Gilbert. 'Fourteen. That's the minimum we need.'

When they went back into the meeting room, the others were already there. Some, like the two elderly sheep, hadn't in fact gone out.

'Right,' said Jefferson, 'we will proceed very simply. Will all those who are prepared to take part in–' he cast around for the right word – 'in the expedition, please raise their hands.'

He could have expected anything, but not what was about to happen, which would remain one of the most beautiful moments of his life. Because every single hand went up in unison: those who had already promised, like Walter Schmitt and the vixens, and all the others too: the badgers, two squirrels, Simone, the three cows, the cat . . . His gaze roved the room and his eyes filled with tears.

'Thank you,' he stammered. 'Thank you. You're wonderful.'

Mr Cousins, the elderly ram, however, was keen to add: 'My wife and I had misgivings because we're likely to be more of a hindrance than a help, but I used to be a doctor and I know the owner of the central pharmacy here in Granville. He will certainly give me some tranquillisers to keep our prisoners quiet in Roland's luggage compartment, at least as far as the border.'

Since Jefferson was too emotional to speak, Gilbert thanked them all. The two of them were going to devise a plan to ensure that everything would be fine-tuned for the big day and that the various roles would be allocated according to everyone's skills. Every one of them would have the chance to make themselves useful.

On leaving, they ran into the cat, who had lingered to photograph the meeting room.

Jefferson said: 'Thank you for agreeing even though we've not spoken to each other this week and . . .'

The cat pointed to his ears with an apologetic little smile.

'Oh, are you deaf?' asked Gilbert.

The cat nodded. Everything became clear: his keeping himself to himself, his habit of staying aloof during the guided tours, his love of photography and his strange way of making macarons.

'But you put your hand up,' said Jefferson, speaking slowly and clearly so the cat could lip-read. 'Did you understand everything I was saying?'

The cat took a notebook out of his pocket, scribbled a few lines and held it out to Jefferson. He'd written: *No, I didn't understand much but since everyone raised their hand, I said to myself that it was probably a good thing and I did the same.*

'Thank you,' said Jefferson.

The cat took back the notebook and added in his neat handwriting: 'By the way, my name's Rupert.'

'Thank you, Rupert,' said Jefferson.

They were on their way back up to their room when the receptionist called them over, a smile on his lips and a twinkle in his eye. 'So how did your Scrabble evening go?'

Perhaps he thought these strange guests could barely read or write.

'It was fun, thank you,' replied Jefferson.

'Did you find any very long words?'

'Yes, I found SOLIDARITY.'

'Oh, no *Z*s, and no *W*s, that can't have given you much.'

'As a matter of fact it did,' said Jefferson. 'It can give you a lot. Good night.'

Roxanne nearly fainted at the other end of the phone when Jefferson told her about their plan. She'd been happy to play along and book the meeting room so they could get together and talk about what Gilbert had seen, but from that to undertaking this mad venture, no! She knew the two men's reputation. They were godless and lawless, armed and capable of firing into the crowd if they felt threatened. Could he just imagine the twenty-eight Globetrotters lying dead on the floor of the apartment? Mr Edgar had always advised the activists to be cautious and he had no hesitation in cancelling any operation that might be risky. He would certainly not have approved of this assault by a bunch of naïve fools. Jefferson was knocked for six, but he didn't back down.

'Probably not,' he replied, 'but Mr Edgar wouldn't like to know either that his killers are wandering around town, their consciences clear, happy to kill anyone as long as they're well paid. And besides, he hadn't been stabbed in the chest with a pair of scissors when he reasoned in that way.'

This time, it was Roxanne's turn to be knocked for six. This little hedgehog, only twenty-eight inches tall, astounded her. She tried again to dissuade him, explaining what would happen, even in the miraculous event that they were successful: there were often customs checks on coaches of animals heading for the border. If they were stopped with two humans trussed up in the baggage compartment, they'd all be sent to prison for years. For life, even.

'When do you want to carry out your attack?' she asked when she realised her warnings were in vain.

'Our trip ends the day after tomorrow,' explained Jefferson. 'Tomorrow, Sunday, we'll draw up our plan, and Monday morning we'll go into action, just before we set off home.'

Roxanne merely sighed noisily down the telephone.

'Take great care. Be very cautious, I implore you,' she said, before hanging up.

13

The programme for the Globetrotters' last day in Granville included attending morning mass at the cathedral, at least for those who wished to do so. In the afternoon, they could choose between a fashion show in a big hotel in the city centre, or a jousting tournament on the canal.

'You go to the mass without me,' said Jefferson. 'I'm going to do a recce around the apartment block. I'll photograph everything. That way we can draw up a precise action plan, like a military operation, you see?'

This was the first rainy day. There was a steady drizzle and the town no longer had a holiday atmosphere. They went their separate ways after breakfast. Gilbert told Jefferson to be on his guard. 'Take care, hedgehog. Promise?'

'Promise,' replied Jefferson, unfurling the black umbrella borrowed from the hotel which was much too big for him. 'And you, remember what Mr Schmitt says about the models if he goes to the fashion show. I'm sorry I'll miss that.'

He walked through the sleeping old town, passing the metal shutters drawn down over the still-closed shops, like eyelids, he said to himself. He headed for the wide avenue, trying to make himself as unobtrusive as possible, checking the numbers. Gilbert had said, 'It's number 44, and the window is on the second floor, just above the entrance, you can't mistake it.' Jefferson walked past the building a first time, almost without daring to look. He took two photos of the street using his phone, one in each direction. At least they showed that the coach could park outside number 44 while the Globetrotters carried out their mission. He carried on for another hundred yards or so, then crossed over the road and turned back, trying to walk with a decisive step, like someone who knows where they're going. Now the rain had become a downpour. It was beating down so hard on the fabric of his umbrella that it sounded like gunfire. His heart beat faster to the rhythm. Arriving at number 44, he stretched up to reach the round doorknob, which he couldn't manage to turn, but when he pushed against the door, he had the pleasant surprise of feeling it give way under the pressure: it was open.

The hallway was particularly uninviting with its grubby yellow walls, greyish staircase, letterboxes plastered with peeling stickers and trampled advertising flyers lying on the floor. Jefferson felt nostalgic for his little cottage on the edge of the forest, the beech trees that would be resplendent with their autumn colours by now, his neat little home. He closed his umbrella and leaned it against the wall, then took photos from every angle: the lift, the stairs, the passageway closed off at one end by a door with a drawing of dustbin on it. He pressed the lift call button, which failed to light up, but the folding metal door opened all the same. He went up to the fourth and last floor, came back down again and made a mental note: *Lift working. Could hold six to eight animals depending on their weight.* Then he set off up the stairs, assessing their width, and went noiselessly up to the second floor. Three doors opened off the landing, which was also a yellowy colour, but only one was on the street side. There was no possible doubt: behind those few inches of wood lived Mr Edgar's murderer, or his accomplice. In any case, a man capable of killing. A shiver ran down Jefferson's spine. There was no name anywhere. Silently, he went right up to the door and pressed his ear to it. At first, he couldn't hear anything and was about to leave, when suddenly, he froze.

There was a noise like cardboard being ripped. Then a man's voice, very low, a voice from beyond the grave. And another, rasping, answering him, but Jefferson couldn't make out the words. He felt his legs turn to jelly. He retreated, inch by inch, convinced that the slightest squeak from his shoes on the floor, the slightest rustle of his trouser legs sounded as loud as a train going through a tunnel.

He made his way down the staircase, fighting the urge to run away as fast as his legs could carry him. It was only thinking about Chuck that stopped him. Once at the bottom, he decided to go and explore the bin area at the far end of the passage. It could serve as a hiding place when they carried out the attack. Go on! Just this little thing, then he'd be able to go back to the hotel satisfied he'd accomplished his mission. He pushed open the door and pinched his nose. It was a little internal courtyard, hemmed in by four windowless walls. The cover of the big black bin was raised, giving off a stench of decomposing refuse. A yellow dustbin, also with the lid off, was overflowing with papers, plastics, boxes and whisky bottles which had no business being there. Jefferson had no desire to hang around. He was just coming out when he heard the door of the lift grate and a man stepped out. Jefferson caught a brief glimpse of his face: it was Red, the man with the beanie.

Jefferson leaped backwards, almost fainting with terror and let out a long, heartrending *'Aaaaaaaaaaaaaaaaaagh!'* as quietly as he could.

Getting a grip on himself, he tried to calm down. The man was very likely on his way out, so all he had to do was wait for him to leave and then go himself. But that is not what happened. He could hear the man cursing as he battled with bulky objects, probably boxes, dropping them, picking them up again and banging against the lift door and the walls. Terrified, Jefferson dived behind the yellow bin and hid. For once, his small size was an advantage.

Now the man was there, in the bin area, less than a few feet away from him, and was chucking the boxes any old how on top of the pile. One of

them, folded, slid behind the bin and Jefferson was hit on the head by the hard edge. But it would have taken a lot more for him to say 'ouch' right then. He pressed his back to the wall and held his breath, his eyes glued to the words on the box: *HD LED TV 48-inch*. The man was furiously trying to fill the bin, thumping and swearing. Jefferson suddenly realised he'd forgotten to turn off his phone. It could ring at any moment and give him away. And the more he said to himself that his phone might ring, the more he was convinced that it *would* ring, that it would do so in the next ten seconds. He slid a hand into his pocket, fished out the phone and began to fiddle with it with trembling hands.

He lost his grip. The dull thud of the phone hitting the concrete floor made the man, who was already half-way out of the door, stop in his tracks. For a moment there was nothing but an unbearable silence, then Jefferson heard the very slow footsteps of the man returning.

'Heeeeelp!' he groaned inwardly and he felt as if all his internal organs were shrinking.

He saw the bin tilt backwards a little and roll away from the wall on its wheels, he saw the scattered boxes that were still concealing him disappear one after the other, removed by invisible hands, then the colossal shape of the man in the beanie appeared. He'd already met him twice, but never up close. His face was pock-marked and his teeth broken, but the most frightening thing about him was his two glassy eyes, devoid of any humanity.

'Well, well, I think I recognise you,' said the man. 'Are you not dear Mr Jefferson?'

'No, my name's Steven,' stammered Jefferson.

'What?' said the man.

'My name's Steven,' he repeated a little louder, amazing himself at his quick reflex. The first name of his cousin had miraculously come to mind.

'Yeah, right,' sniggered the man. 'Like I'm going to believe you!'

And his hand came down on the scruff of Jefferson's neck, grabbing his collar and his skin.

Jefferson struggled and tried to bite him, but the man's grip paralysed his entire upper body. He felt himself being lifted up and carried off. The man had picked up his phone in passing and retrieved the forgotten umbrella from the hallway. He entered the lift, holding his prey at arm's length to avoid being kicked.

'Press two, that's where we're going,' he

commanded Jefferson. He pushed the button with his little forefinger.

'Hey, Mackie, look!'

When the man with the beanie showed off his catch, his tall, thin companion's hollow laugh must have echoed throughout the building.

'What on earth's that?'

His voice was incredibly deep. His prominent Adam's apple yo-yoed up and down his stubbly neck.

'It's our friend Jefferson. Don't you recognise him?' rasped beanie man, pointing to the table where there lay a copy of *The Daily Trumpet*, the one with Jefferson holding his blueberry tart on the front page. 'It's him, isn't it?'

The tall, thin one was sprawled in an armchair, busy reading a brochure. The swollen veins in his hands, his predatory jaw – everything about him betrayed a cruel and jumpy nature. At his feet lay a flat-screen TV, a jumble of cables, remains of packaging, bits of bubble-wrap.

'Yeah, it looks like him,' he said. 'Doesn't have the quiff any more, but it looks like him. So you killed Mr Edgar, did you? If they're accusing you, you must have done it, right? Who else could it have been?'

He laughed at his own joke. Unlike the beanie guy's expressionless eyes, his friend's were fiery – the eyes of a madman.

'My name's Steven,' Jefferson repeated, convinced that his survival depended on this lie, and then he felt the first blow.

The beanie guy had altered his grip and now held him by his shirt collar, under his throat, still at arm's length. His hand was so broad that the slap stung half of Jefferson's head, and his right ear began to buzz.

'Say that again . . .'

'My name's Steven,' insisted Jefferson, and the hand came down again.

'What were you doing down there, hiding among the bins?'

He didn't reply.

'Is that his phone?' asked Mackie, without moving from his chair. 'Chuck it over!'

He soon discovered the dozen or so photos.

'What's all this? What are you playing at?'

'I . . . I'm studying architecture,' said Jefferson. 'I take photos of . . .'

'Arti ... what?' thundered Mackie. 'Artichokes? Are you taking the mickey out of us? Look, Red, he's taken pictures of the street, the hallway, the staircase, everything. What are you up to? How did you find this place, eh?'

'*You* heard,' echoed Red. 'How did you get here?'

'By chance,' began Jefferson. 'I was in the neighbourhood and I ...'

The hand rose again, and this time the effect was like a tremendous firework, but dark. And astonishingly quite pretty. A sort of spectacular final bouquet with the last rocket that shoots up very high, vanishes for a moment, then explodes even higher and sends out magnificent sprays that explode further. Then he felt himself being flung to the floor. He heard the crack his limbs and head made as they hit the ground, but it didn't hurt. 'My name's Steven,' he said to himself again, and then there was nothing but a big, black, silent sky.

The ray of light filtering under the door was enough to tell him that he was in a broom cupboard. How long had he been there? He had no idea. In the half-dark, he could make out a plastic bucket and a floor cloth. The smell of mould was suffocating. His entire body ached: his knees, his head, his back and his hips. His elbow in particular hurt like mad. The whistling had taken on a lower tone but continued to deafen his right ear. Moving a little, he became aware that he'd wet his trousers again, but in the situation he found himself in, this annoyance seemed of secondary importance.

The voices of the two men reached him without his having to strain to hear. They were setting up the TV while chatting, and that resulted in a strange dialogue.

'Yeah, without the cable, there's no signal, no wonder.'

'The set comes with a router, doesn't it?'

'You hit him a bit hard! We can't question him any more.'

'No worries, he'll wake up. Pass me the remote.'

'I reckon he ran away to avoid jail, I do.'

'That's what they say in the paper.'

'Set it to terrestrial . . . *terrestrial* I said!'

'Are you certain he's the one we nearly ran over?'

'Certain. And he gets the whole thing, the crafty little blighter.'

At times, there were silences, and then they'd be off again, 'Terrestrial, I said! Are you deaf or what?'

'He found us. Dunno how, but he found us. If we let him go, he'll grass on us . . . Which end? The yellow? What are the others for, then? It's a load of rubbish, this thing.'

'I reckon we should wring 'is neck.'

At these words, Jefferson suddenly forgot all his aches and pains. His mind was as alert as if a bucket of cold water had been thrown over his face. Had he heard correctly? 'Wring 'is neck'? He desperately tried to reassure himself. They were probably going to ring some friend called *Iznek* to help them sort out their wretched TV. He didn't understand what the problem was, but that must be it: they were going to call their friend to sort out the cables.

He waited, almost passing out with terror. Was he dreaming or were these two humans really planning to murder him? Was he destined to die here, in this smelly cupboard, far from his loved ones, without being able to say goodbye to anyone? He thought of his sister Chelsea, of Gilbert. His heart bled. He groaned softly. *'Ohhhhh . . .'*

The conversation continued on the other side of the door, both calm and terrifying.

'I think so too. Gotta get rid of him. But that's your job. Why's there no sound? There's a picture but no sound. Me, I already did the badger in, remember. So now, it's your turn.'

This last sentence was spoken by Mackie, the tall, skinny one. So he was the one who'd killed dear Mr Edgar in cold blood.

'It's because you've got it on mute, stupid!' replied Red. 'Pass the remote. The thing is, what do we do with the creature afterwards? I'd happily throw him . . .'

Just then, the deafening sound of the TV, on maximum volume, filled the room.

'. . . *only seven minutes left until the final whistle, it's going to be tough for the Greens, but they've already shown several times this season* . . .' said the commentator.

'Turn it down, stupid!' barked Mackie.

The sound stopped abruptly.

'It works!' said Red. 'Yeah, I'd stuff him at the bottom of the big bin. What do you think? That's where he was, by the bins. 'Spect he likes it there.'

'What time do your bin men come?'

'At six in the morning. I know. They make a hell of a racket.'

There was another long silence, then Red's croaky voice. 'Right. You stay here tonight. I don't want to do it on my own, and I'll deal with it in the morning,

177

at around five. I'll do like my father used to do with the rabbits.'

'Ah ha, and what did your father do with the rabbits?'

'You take them by their hind legs, you let them dangle, and you stun them with a blow to the back of the neck. The rabbit stops struggling, it freezes, it starts trembling. And then you stick the knife in its throat, in the right place so that it bleeds heavily.'

'You'll get blood everywhere.'

'Nah, I'd do it over the bathtub. Then we'll smuggle him downstairs and bung him at the bottom of the bin.'

'They'll see him.'

'Nah, there's not much of him. And anyway, it's mechanical. They attach the bin, it tilts up and everything's tipped into the truck. They don't even see what's inside.'

Jefferson cowered at the back of the cupboard, as if putting a few more inches between him and the men could ward off the danger. He rested his head on his knees and stayed like that for a long time, hunched up, like a defenceless and terrified little animal.

Then, slowly, he managed to think again. So his

short life was going to end in the bathroom of a strange apartment in Granville, in the Land of the Humans. He said to himself that he'd had a good life. He'd been lucky: a happy childhood, loyal friends. He'd laughed a lot, read some wonderful books, listened to music. He'd started studying for a degree. OK, there were still a few little things he hadn't done. He'd have liked to have a girlfriend, for example, before dying. That yes, that was a bit pathetic, to die before ever having a girlfriend. *Drat, I'm too young to die!* he said to himself, and his eyes welled up.

The two men were silent. They were channel-surfing every possible channel, and there were a lot of them, in all languages. They were incapable of watching the same one for more than fifteen seconds.

'I'm starving,' said Mackie after about an hour. 'I'm gonna grab myself a pizza from Nino's. What d'you want?'

'Pepperoni!' replied Red. 'A large one.'

'A three cheese for me,' murmured Jefferson, but it didn't even make him laugh.

He heard the front door open and close, and it occurred to him that he might be able to escape. Red thought he was still unconscious. All he needed to do was slip out of the cupboard and leave. He stood up, taking care not to make any noise. His legs could barely support him. He pushed against the door and realised that it was hopeless. It only opened from the outside. He sat down again. The best thing was to keep still. He remembered the story of Tom Thumb, where the giant decides to wait until the next morning to slit the throats of the seven children, and then changes his mind in the middle of the night because he's hungry. If Red felt peckish, he'd probably make do with going to the fridge, but if Jefferson became too much of a nuisance, he could very well change his plans and commit the worst.

There was still Gilbert and the Globetrotters. What would they decide to do when he didn't come back? The attack was to take place on the Monday morning. If they kept to that plan, they might capture the killers, but he, Jefferson, would be long dead, buried somewhere under a mountain of refuse. And his body would never be found.

When Mackie returned after around fifteen minutes, a delicious aroma of warm pizza dough filtered under the door. Jefferson, who loved pizza, would gladly have shared it with the two killers. Except he found it hard to imagine the conversation:

'*A little hot sauce, my dear Jefferson, er, my dear Steven, I mean?*'

'*With pleasure, dear Red, you're too kind.*'

'*Oh please, it's your last meal, so it's only natural we should pamper you.*'

He heard the clatter of plates in the kitchen. Despite the TV, he managed to follow every detail of the evening from the sounds: the toilet flushing, bottles of beer being opened, clinking together, the rattle of knives and forks against the plates, the laughter, burps and yawns.

He curled up in a ball and fell asleep from exhaustion and all the emotion.

When he woke up, it was pitch dark. Silence reigned in the apartment. What time could it be? Red had said he'd deal with it at around five o'clock in the morning. Jefferson's stomach was churning with fear.

He told himself that Gilbert wouldn't abandon him. They'd made a pact once, in their hut. They'd made a little cut in their arms with a pointed twig and mingled their blood, and they'd sworn to help each other out until death. Gilbert had clowned around and laughed a lot when saying the oath, but he had sworn. He also told himself, unfortunately, that they were only teenage vows, and that teenage vows don't count, that real life makes people forget them.

There was a church somewhere nearby, and Jefferson heard the bells ring, a long way off. Was it two or three o'clock in the morning? He promised himself he'd listen more carefully the next time. He frequently shifted his position so as not to get stiff: sitting, lying on one side, then on the other, curled up in a ball, lying on his back with his legs in the air against the partition. When the bells rang again, he held his breath and listened: one, two, three, four. It was four o'clock.

From that moment, he was nothing but a ball of anxiety. Never would the Globetrotters attack during the night. They'd all be snoring in the Majestic's soft beds, except Gilbert who was probably going frantic, waiting for daybreak. There was still the hope that Red and Mackie, drunk on beer, would oversleep.

This slender hope was dashed on the third chime of five o'clock when the sound of an alarm clock broke the silence of the apartment. That rogue Red had thought of everything. He'd set his alarm to kill, the way normal people set it to get up for work or to catch a train!

Jefferson heard them getting dressed, muttering words he didn't understand. Then there was Red's lazy step in the passage, the door of the broom cupboard opening . . . Panic triggered an instinctive reflex in him: pretend he was in a deep sleep. Some animals feign death to escape it! The predator doesn't want carrion that's already cold! He lay spread-eagled on the floor, his mouth open, tongue lolling. He knew his ruse had no chance of succeeding, but what else could he do?

This pathetic performance had no effect on Red who grabbed him by his ankles and swung him up with disconcerting ease. Jefferson's wallet and a tin of throat pastilles fell out of his pockets. At that point he figured he'd had it, and within a second he went from frozen to frenzied. He wouldn't allow himself to be done in just like that! He wanted to live! He screamed: 'Help! Help!' at the top of his voice, and fought back. He refused to dangle as Red had hoped. On the contrary, he wriggled like an eel and managed to strike him in the face and in the stomach.

Red hadn't been expecting this sudden rebellion,

but what worried him most were Jefferson's piercing shrieks. He'd alert the neighbours, the idiot!

'Will you shut it!' he hissed furiously and punched Jefferson three times in the head with his clenched left fist – three rapid, violent blows.

Jefferson, dazed, turned the volume down, but continued to struggle. He even managed to grab Red's crotch through his trousers and squeeze with all his strength.

'Ooowwww!' groaned Red, doubled over with pain and with rage. He hurled Jefferson to the floor and kicked the living daylights out of him.

'What the hell are you doing?' asked Mackie, who came in doing up his belt buckle.

'He got me in the nuts . . .' whined Red.

Mackie sniggered.

'Well, make it quick! I wanna drop into my place on the way to work. I'll go an' get you the knife.'

Hearing the word 'knife', Jefferson leaped up and made a beeline for the front door. He already had his hand on the knob when Red caught him.

'Help!' he yelled again, 'Help me!'

This time, Red wasn't in the mood for laughing at all. He floored Jefferson with a heavy blow to the temple. Jefferson lost consciousness for a few seconds and, when he came to, he was dangling over the bathtub, held by the ankles in one hand, and he was vomiting. Mackie was handing Red a big kitchen knife. Their words echoed horribly in the tiled bathroom.

'D'you know what to do?'

'Of course. Give it here.'

'D'you want me to hold him?'

'Yeah. I can't knock him out, the slime ball.'

Mackie placed one foot on the edge of the bathtub and wedged Jefferson's body against his knee to keep him still, then twisted his arm behind his back. Now, Jefferson was completely defenceless.

'Help!' he tried to shout, but all that came out of his mouth was a vague gargling sound and a pathetic *'Aaaaaaargh.'*

Then there was a silence.

'What's that?' asked Mackie, on the alert.

The *knock, knock* was almost inaudible. All three of them strained to hear: the two humans with a faint anxiety, Jefferson with insane hope.

Knock, knock again, a little louder, at the front door. Louder still, and after a pause: *knock, knock*. It echoed through the sleeping building.

'Go and see!' muttered Red, and Mackie tiptoed

off down the passage. A few seconds went by. Mackie was probably looking through the spyhole.

He came back.

Red shot him a questioning look. 'What is it?'

Mackie pulled a face and spread his hands. 'A fox . . .'

'Don't open the door. Wait.'

Red was holding the knife to Jefferson's throat. He could feel its cold tip on his skin. The two humans stood stock-still, listening. The pause lasted for around ten seconds. The knocking had stopped.

'Go on,' said Mackie, tightening his grip.

14

The door was made of hard wood and was at least three centimetres thick. So when it gave way, it sounded as if a shell had exploded inside the apartment. The wood shattered with a resounding crash, followed immediately by loud shouts. 'My shoulder! Ouch! My shoulder!'

Walter Schmitt, who'd smashed into the door with the force of a cannonball, was only able to stop when he hit the opposite wall, at the other end of the passage, and now he was kneeling on the floor, groaning. 'Owww, I've shattered my shoulder, dammit!'

Red and Mackie stared at him in amazement, but they didn't have time to wonder for long at the incongruous presence of a ruddy-faced, tearful boar. The twenty-six other animals poured through the doorway and launched into the attack.

'FIND HIM!' yelled Gilbert.

The duck and Clarissa the hen, accompanied by the quickest animals, dispersed through all the rooms shouting, 'Jeff! Are you here?'

'Mr Jefferson! Are you here?'

'Yoo hoo! Anyone here?'

It was Clarissa who was the first to burst into the bathroom. She bumped into Mackie as he was coming out.

'They're heeeeeeeeeeeere!' she screamed.

'What's this circus?' shouted Mackie, kicking her in the chest.

'CHARGE!' commanded Gilbert.

The nanny goat and her husband soared into the air side by side. They jumped over Clarissa and charged headlong at Mackie, whose head hit the corner of the washbasin. He sank to the floor.

Red had dropped Jefferson into the bathtub. He turned to face his assailants, holding a knife with a bloodstained blade at arm's length.

'Ladies, gentlemen, is there a problem?' he asked in his usual sardonic tone, but incredulity was written all over his face.

'Noooooooooo!' yelled Gilbert on discovering the

blood-spattered Jefferson unmoving at the bottom of the bathtub.

'*Oh yes,*' replied Red icily.

He'd have done better to hold his tongue and keep an eye on his attackers, because little Mrs Pearl had slipped unnoticed behind all of them, hauled herself up onto the edge of the bathtub and was brandishing a cast-iron saucepan (borrowed from the hotel) above Red's head.

'Wa . . . Watch owww . . .' stuttered Mackie, coming round.

'What?' asked Red.

'The squi—the squi . . .'

'DESTROY!' yelled Roland, who'd taken over control of the operation from his cousin.

The saucepan came down on Red's skull and he fell on top of his friend.

'Did I do that?' asked Mrs Pearl, watching him crumple.

She stared at the pan in her hand.

'It's the first time in my life that I've knocked someone out . . . did you see me, Gustave?'

'I saw you, darling . . .' Mr Pearl congratulated her. 'Well done.'

'IMMOBILISE!' shouted Roland.

Then the Globetrotters' heavyweights launched into action. The cow, her two young nieces and Mrs Schmitt charged into the bathroom and the four of them landed on top of the two killers.

'*Ooowww!*' said Mackie.

'*Ooowww!*' added Red.

Mr Cousins, the elderly sheep doctor, was already crouching beside Jefferson in the bathtub, and Gilbert had joined them.

'Jeff! Jeff! Talk to me.'

The doctor lay Jefferson on his back and placed his ear to his chest.

'He's breathing and his heart's beating. That's one good thing. Pass me the showerhead, please.'

The bathroom was crowded with silent animals. The only sound was Simone's sobs as she stretched over the others' heads.

'Will he live?' she burbled.

Doctor Cousins rinsed Jefferson's face so as better to see his wounds and everyone was surprised to hear him moan.

'Yes, I think he'll live. But we arrived in the nick of time. The knife must have slipped. Here, Gilbert, wrap this in your handkerchief in case he'd like to keep it as a souvenir.'

'What is it?'

'It's an ear. But don't worry. It's more decorative than anything else. He'll manage very well without it.'

When Jefferson came round, he saw a dozen friendly faces leaning over him: the delighted expression of his friend Gilbert, the affectionate ones of the badgers, the cat's look of astonishment, and the faces of Clarissa and the two vixens (looking serious for once), and all the rest.

'I'm very happy that you came,' he said. 'Thank you.'

For someone who was retired, the doctor had a lot to do in the minutes that followed. He'd come prepared, having bought everything that was necessary for a medical emergency from the central pharmacy. He put a dressing on Jefferson's ear and bandaged his head, then gave him a pill.

'This will help you sleep,' he explained.

Then he moved on to the two killers who were on the brink of suffocating to death, crushed under the weight of the cow and her nieces. They raised themselves up just enough for him to be able to jab a syringe into their buttocks.

'Good night, gentlemen,' he said. 'I am the sandman, do you recognise me?'

They had both lost their sense of humour. Mackie struggled hard, but his eyes closed despite his efforts. As for Red, he was already smiling blissfully, which wasn't a pretty sight because of his rotten teeth.

'Could you take care of my husband, doctor?' Mrs Schmitt asked shyly, getting to her feet.

They had almost forgotten the good Walter, who hadn't moved from the hallway. He was sitting doubled over with his back against the wall, nursing his right arm.

'I so wanted to take part in the fight, but I've hurt my shoulder. That wretched door was solid! I'm sorry.'

'Don't be silly,' Gilbert comforted him while the doctor put his arm in a sling. 'Quite the opposite, you were terrific. We'd never have done it without you.'

The next-door neighbour, woken by the noise, was standing in his doorway in his pyjamas, open-mouthed at the sight of twenty-eight animals following one another out through the smashed door. They all greeted him politely before heading down the stairs. One of the vixens whispered, 'It's a dream, sir, just a dream.'

He wondered briefly whether he should call the police, but when he saw the two pigs, Roland and Gilbert, dragging Mackie's body by the feet and bundling him into the lift, he decided the fox was right: it was just one of those weird dreams that you sometimes have in the early hours. And he went back to bed. After taking a sedative.

The Globetrotters' coach was parked directly outside number 44. At that hour, the street was empty. A fine drizzle made the road glisten. The two rogues had been trussed up by Rupert the cat, who was an expert on knots, and the animals slid them right to the back of the luggage compartment. They built a wall of suitcases and bags to hide them.

They turned the back of the coach into a sick bay. Mr Schmitt was given cushions to support his shoulder and soften the jolts. Jefferson, knocked out by the pill Doctor Cousins had given him, was able to stretch out over two seats, nice and snug beneath a blanket, his head on a travel pillow. To those who asked if he was all right, he simply replied in a sleepy voice, 'Yes, but I didn't return the umbrella to the hotel, and that worries me . . .' as if that were of the slightest importance right then.

They thought these were the only two casualties, but at the last minute there was a third. While transferring the captives to the coach, Roland had slipped on the kerbstone and twisted his left ankle so badly that within a few minutes it had swollen to the size of a mini football. Doctor Cousins immediately diagnosed a nasty sprain, and there was no question of the poor driver taking the wheel again.

'No problem with the wheel,' he said, laughing wryly, 'but there's no way I can work the clutch, and I have no intention of driving three hundred miles in first gear!'

They climbed aboard anyway, and when they were all settled, Roland stood up on one leg.

'Right, who can take my place and drive?'

This very simple question threw the group into a panic, especially because they really needed to get away quickly.

'I haven't got a licence,' said Simone.

'Nor have I,' said Mrs Hild.

'Nor have I,' mimicked the cat.

'I haven't driven a motor vehicle for twelve years,' said her husband.

'I can't reach the pedals,' said Clarissa.

'We only have a little electric car,' said the squirrels. 'So a coach . . .'

They all had a good reason not to sit in the driver's seat, and when everyone had spoken, all eyes turned to the only one who had said nothing.

'Gilbert, my boy,' began Roland, massaging his ankle, 'over to you! We're cousins and we look alike. Put on my jacket and cap. If there's an identity check, your name is Roland. Sorted! Off we go!'

'What do you mean, "Sorted! Off we go"? You're forgetting one detail, a stupid little thing.'

'What stupid little thing?'

'It's that I don't know how to drive! I know the *Highway Code* by heart, but I've never driven!'

'Ta-dah! I'll sit beside you and help you. Come on! There's no other option! We have to leave!'

Under normal circumstances, Roland's suggestion would have met with downright refusal, but the Globetrotters had just lived through a night that was so crazy that they'd lost their common sense. They began to clap their hands and chant: 'Gil-bert! Gil-bert!'

'OK,' he sighed, putting on his cousin's cap. 'You asked for it.'

He drove the first hundred and fifty yards scraping the tyres against the kerb.

'Straighten up!' groaned Roland, sitting next to him. 'Straighten up, there's already a smell of burnt rubber!'

Then he spent the next mile trying to change

gear. Roland barked instructions: 'Clutch! Clutch! The left pedal! Faster! No, slow down! Yes, you've stalled, not surprising! That's good, but you're accelerating too hard! Clutch! No, you're not in first, that's neutral, so you can't move. Push the gearstick as far as you can! Push! Push! Push! Clutch! Not so fast! No, you can't see anything because you've got your cap over your eyes, push it up! Start up again! Accelerate! Clutch! No, don't hoot! Clutch! Yessss! Gently! Brake! Brake!'

The coach juddered, stopped suddenly and lurched forwards, the windscreen wipers went crazy, the engine stalled, roared, the gearbox screeched in pain. When Gilbert finally managed to change up to second, the coach erupted and the Globetrotters all started chanting 'Gil-bert! Gil-bert!' again.

Luckily there was little dawn traffic and they were able to extricate themselves from the town having hit only three parked cars and scraped the entire side of the coach against a wall which, according to Gilbert, had suddenly jumped out in front of him. As for the roundabouts, he drove onto them, cutting up everyone else and often driving around twice before turning off. He finally managed to get into third gear amid indescribable excitement. The yellow

coach sped through the countryside that sparkled in the rain. They wisely avoided the motorway. Gilbert would rather have died than venture onto it. Gripping the wheel, the poor creature was dripping with sweat.

'I'll never make it . . .' he groaned, but there was a very long, straight stretch where he managed to get up to forty miles an hour, where no manoeuvres needed to be made. The animals fussed over him: one of the vixens came and mopped his brow with her handkerchief, Mrs Hild brought him a cup of hot tea and Clarissa massaged his shoulders.

Things were going better but they got stuck behind a tractor for a good fifteen minutes. Gilbert didn't dare overtake it for ages, and when he did make up his mind to do so, his jaw clenched, the engine roaring, the Globetrotters were almost ecstatic. 'Gil-bert! Gil-bert!' they chanted over and over until they'd passed the poor astonished farmer. Many of them hugged one another.

A young calf, sitting right at the back, came forward to inform them that a little red car with a bicycle on top had been following them since Granville. It stopped when they stopped and set off again when they did. Strange, wasn't it?

'No time to deal with it,' replied Roland. 'Keep

going, keep going!' They didn't stop either to eat or drink or for a pee. Their dearest wish was to reach the border as quickly as possible. How did Gilbert manage to get his little group that far? It was a miracle, but he did it. Well, almost.

They were just a few miles away from the frontier on the country road when a police car overtook them. The flashing lights and the police officer's arm at the window left no room for doubt: inspection!

Gilbert was slow to react.

'Brake! Braaaaaaake!' yelled Roland and the coach came to a halt on the grass verge, within a foot of the police car's bumper.

The engine stalled with a final judder and there was a deathly silence.

15

The police officer who boarded the coach looked as if he was in no mood to joke. His grim expression, thin lips and steely blue eyes made them fear the worst. He wore a bullet-proof vest over his uniform and a peaked cap with the word 'CUSTOMS' on it.

'Good day, ladies and gentlemen,' he said, raising one finger to his peak.

'Good day, officer!' chorused the twenty-seven animals.

'I presume you know why we are stopping you?' asked the police officer.

'Um ... no,' stammered Gilbert who was sweating profusely, still clutching the wheel. 'I mean, yes, sort of ...'

'We've been following you for a few minutes

and you have broken a sort of world record: in five miles you have committed seventeen traffic offences.'

'I'm sorry, I . . .'

'But you're very fortunate that we're not the traffic police. We're customs officers and that's not our business. On the other hand, we would like to inspect the bags in your luggage compartment. Would you open it up, please?'

'Of course, with pleasure, um . . . have you got the key, Roland?'

In the meantime, Roland's ankle, resting on a cool bag, had swollen to the size of a football. He twisted and turned as he rummaged in his many jacket and trouser pockets one by one.

'Let's see, where's that key . . . it's not here . . . not in this one either . . . maybe in this one . . . no . . . oh, this is silly, isn't it? . . . Ah, here it is! . . . Oh no it isn't, it's the key to my bicycle shed . . . yes, because I've started riding an electric bike and, given the price, I don't fancy having it stolen, you know? Have you tried an electric bike, officer? Oh, I swear it's amazing. Going uphill you feel as if . . .'

The police officer's expression hardened and his right shoe began to tap the coach floor impatiently.

The Globetrotters were quiet and in the silence, a dull *thump* could be heard. It sounded like knocking coming from inside a crate. Then came a distant shout, 'Open up . . .'

The voice was muffled but audible. Everyone had heard it, except the police officer who was probably a little hard of hearing.

'Open up . . . lemme outta here!' said the voice, barely louder.

And again, *thump thump*. Which of the two murderers had woken up? And how did he manage to bang when they'd both been thoroughly trussed up? Most likely with his head. In any case, it couldn't have happened at a worse moment.

How did Clarissa come up with such a brilliant idea? Thinking about it afterwards, she was astonished herself. She'd had the brainwave of repeatedly banging the side of the coach with her fist. Then she began to sing: 'Open up! Ooooopen! Open up, lemme outta here! Ah, ah!'

Straight away, the two calves, Mrs Cousins and Mrs Pearl sang along too: 'Open up! Ooooopen! Open up, let us outta here! Ah ah!'

The male voices joined in, an octave lower, and fists hammered the metal sides of the coach, *thump,*

thump: 'Open up! Oooooopen! Open up, let us outta here! Ah ah! Ah aaaaah!'

But they couldn't keep repeating that completely idiotic chorus for ever. They needed verses, and that's where Mr Hild came into his own. The fate of his travel companions depended on his inventive talents. He made up such a clever line that it sounded as though it had always existed: 'In his dingy jail, Ol' Guy Fawkes did wail . . .'

And it rhymed! The entire coach burst into the chorus, banging harder and harder with their fists: 'Open up! Ooooopen! Open up, lemme outta here! Ah!'

Mr Hild improvised a brilliant second verse in his deep bass voice: 'In their prison cell, two lil' princes did yell . . .'

'Open up! Ooooopen! Open up, let us outta here!' bawled the twenty-seven Globetrotters, desperately trying to drown out the banging from the luggage compartment, which had started up again. 'Ah, ah! Ah, aaaaah! Get us outta this rathole!'

'The key!' commanded the police officer, disconcerted to say the least.

Roland, who'd just found it, accidentally dropped

it under his seat, and Gilbert threw himself down on his stomach to retrieve it.

'Oh, it's so annoying. I touched it with my fingertips and that pushed it further away! I can't reach it. You wouldn't have a knitting needle or something like that on you, would you?'

Roland continued to distract the police officer by harping on about the electric bicycle, and because the others were singing their heads off, he had to shout to make himself heard, 'There are several settings, you see, so you can adjust the level of assistance from the motor. If it's a gentle hill and you're warmed up, you can ask for minimum assistance, but as soon as the going gets hard, or if you're feeling a bit tired, then you can . . .'

The customs officer mopped his forehead with his handkerchief. In his twenty-year career, he'd never come across such a weird bunch. What with the lecture on the advantages of the electric bike, the racket, the wild singing and the lost key, he felt the situation was becoming increasingly out of control. Besides, this was the first time he'd ever been asked if he had a *knitting needle or something like that* on him. At that point, he might have been about to just give up and abandon all thought of an inspection. But unfortunately his colleague suddenly appeared on the footboard.

'Chief, I simply tried the handle of the luggage compartment . . . and it's not locked.' The customs officer glared furiously at the animals and got down from the coach. The singing stopped.

Gilbert stood up and threw his arms up in the air. That meant: *Well, we did our best, but I think that now we're done for.*

'Are the police here because of my umbrella?' asked Jefferson, completely out of it. 'I'm so sorry, it's all my fault . . . I wanted to take it back but . . .'

Mr Schmitt tried to reassure him. 'No, no, it's nothing to do with your brolly, Jefferson. Go back to sleep.'

All those sitting on the verge side of the coach pressed their noses to the windows to watch what would happen next. It wasn't difficult to foresee: in a few moments' time, the police officers would discover the two humans trussed up in the luggage compartment and it would be a disaster. The Globetrotters would all be handcuffed, thrown into a police van and taken back to Granville to be questioned, sentenced and imprisoned in groups of four in dark dungeons. They could well be bawling 'Open up, open up, get us outta here' for years, but no one would come to their rescue. That was what was going to happen.

Since his cousin was unable to put any weight on his foot, Gilbert got off the coach in his place, resigned to the worst. But, as he often liked to say, the worst is never certain. The chief was about to open up the baggage compartment when something utterly astonishing happened: a mountain bike hurtling at full speed appeared between the embankment and the coach. It brushed past Gilbert and wove between the two police officers. The young woman riding it had short, dishevelled hair that was . . . orange. She reached out, whisked off the chief's cap, plonked it back-to-front on her own head and pedalled like a bat out of hell in the direction of Granville. She put everything she had into it, elbows wide, her nose on the handlebars.

The police officer swore and yelled several insults, the least offensive being, 'Oh, the minx!'

He set off after her, flanked by his colleague. But on foot, they had no chance of catching the fugitive. So they ran back to their car as if their lives depended on it, leaped in and did a U-turn that made the tyres squeal. Humiliation gave them wings. That cheeky miss was going to pay dearly for her audacity. Oh yes, very dearly!

'Should we wait here for you, officers?' asked Gilbert in his most innocent voice.

'Move it!' shouted the police officer through his lowered window. And that meant: *Get out of here, I've had enough of you!*

The Globetrotters didn't wait to be told twice. They went back to their places and those who hadn't had time to do so found themselves thrown into their seats as the coach abruptly lurched forward. At the back the two vixens turned around to see whether Roxanne would get away.

'She's still pedalling,' said one.

'Oh, goodness, they've caught up with her!' said the other.

'Yes, she's zigzagging to shake them off, but she's had it.'

'Yes, that's it, they've almost got her.'

They were quiet for a moment and then they began to shriek excitedly.

'What's happening? What's happening?' asked the Globetrotters.

'She's going faster!'

'Wow, what's she doing?'

'She's riding up the embankment! She's gone into the woods!'

'On her bike?'

'Yes, on her bike! She's vanished!'

'Are they following her?'

'Of course not. They can't.'

'What are they doing?'

'Nothing. Oh yes: the one who's still got his cap has just flung it on the ground.'

A great cry went up in the coach: 'Yesssssssssssssssssss!'

Then came the song that had now become their anthem:

'Open up! Open up! Get us outta here! Ah, ah! Ah, aaaaah!'

At the border, they were waved through as easily as when they'd been travelling in the other direction, a week earlier. They were barely across it when they allowed themselves a brief halt at a service station to have something to eat, stretch their legs and also so that Mr Cousins could discreetly administer a little booster jab to the two clandestine travellers, to keep them quiet for a few more hours.

They set off again at nightfall.

Many of them fell asleep, their heads on their jackets or their travel pillows, the Cousins with their brand-new tartan blanket over their knees. Some of them began to read, or to chat quietly with their neighbour. Mr Schmitt cradled his right elbow in his left hand and moaned softly. 'We'll be there soon, darling, don't worry,' soothed his wife. Jefferson was sleeping like a log. At the wheel, poor Gilbert was close to exhaustion. His back was hunched, his eyelids grew heavier and heavier – driving at night was a new challenge.

'In the *Highway Code* it says that you shouldn't drive for more than three hours in a row, and I've been driving for how many? At least fourteen, haven't I?'

Roland kept his eyes on the road and talked to him all the time.

'You're doing really well … yes, keep your headlights on … let that car overtake you, go on, keep to the left … that's good … that's very good … now dip your lights … are you thirsty?'

Gilbert wasn't driving fast and it was almost three o'clock in the morning when the Globetrotters' little yellow coach reached its destination and parked on the gravel in front of the police station, which was dark, except for a lamp with a mesh guard in front of the main gate. Roland got out of the coach, hopped over to the bell and pressed the button.

'Yes?' asked a man's voice.

'Good evening. My name's Roland,' he said. 'I work for Globetrotters travel, you know, the coaches . . .'

'Yes . . . ?'

'Well, I've just parked our coach in front of this police station. Inside, there are twenty-seven animals who were on a tour to the Land of the Humans . . .'

'Yes . . . ?'

'Yes, and among these animals, there's Jefferson, the hedgehog accused of murdering Mr Edgar, the badger. But he's not the killer. The real killer is tied up in the luggage compartment with his accomplice. We've brought them back to hand over to you.'

The entryphone was silent for a few seconds, then: 'Can you repeat what you have just said, please?'

Roland did so.

'Stay where you are.'

When the policeman, a huge Great Dane, boarded the coach, accompanied by a colleague, they were surprised to find all the passengers asleep, heads thrown back or resting on their neighbour's shoulder.

Some were snoring gently. The driver himself was asleep with his head on the wheel, a smile on his lips.

'He looks very young, your driver,' muttered the policeman, moved by this peaceful sight. 'Has he got his licence?'

'Yes,' mumbled Roland, 'I mean . . . no.'

'Right, we'll see about that later. Where's Jefferson?'

Roland walked ahead of him down the aisle to the back of the coach. The two policemen drew their service pistols and pointed them at the young hedgehog. Jefferson lay across two seats, his head wrapped in a bandage that had a red stain where his ear had been. He opened one eye, and then two. His chin began to wobble.

'Don't shoot . . . I-I'll buy another one, I promise . . . I'll replace it . . .'

16

When Jefferson woke up properly, he couldn't see any gun being pointed at him by a threatening policeman. Nor did he see a kitchen knife being brandished by a human about to slit his throat like a farmed rabbit, nor even the accusing finger of the manager of the Majestic come to demand the forgotten umbrella. He saw only the friendly smile of a partridge nurse leaning over him. Her eyes, magnified by thick spectacle lenses, took up her entire face.

'So, Mr Jefferson, how are you feeling?'

'I feel fine,' he said.

That was the truth. He was floating in a pleasant drowsiness and nothing hurt. The nurse lowered her voice. 'Could I have your autograph?'

'My autograph? Er . . . why?'

She helped him to sit up, wedged the pillow

behind his back and took a little spiral notebook and a pen out of her nurse's tunic.

'Here, please.'

He wrote his name on the first page: *Jefferson*.

'This is my first ever autograph,' he admitted, slightly awed.

'Oh, really? Well I don't think it will be the last. I'll let people know that you're awake. Be prepared to sign a lot more.'

As she was about to go out of the room, she changed her mind and trotted back over to him.

'Could you give me another one, please? I'm taking advantage, aren't I? But it's for my mum. She's full of admiration for you.'

She dashed off before he had a chance to ask her what he was doing in hospital. He wiggled his toes and moved his feet and legs. Everything was working normally. He was able to wave his arms without any difficulty. He shook his head from side to side and then nodded up and down. That was when he felt something heavy on top. He ran his hand over his head and found it was encased in a bandage that was knotted under his chin. It was like a sort of hood. Exploring higher, he touched his short quiff, which

was beginning to grow back. They'd cut a hole to let it through.

The nurse was right. Ten minutes hadn't gone by when Gilbert burst into the room.

'Hello, hedgehog! Oh, wow, you look like an Easter egg! Can I take a photo?'

'If you like. The nurse has just asked me for my autograph. What's going on?'

'What's going on is that you're now a celebrity, my friend!'

'A celebrity? You're going to have to explain. Ten days ago I was public enemy number one, and now ... How long have I been here, by the way? What's wrong with my head? What day is it?'

'It's Wednesday morning. You slept all day yesterday. A little smile please?'

Gilbert took a dozen snaps then sat on the edge of the bed.

'Right, I'll tell you the whole story. Where are you up to? I mean, what's the last thing you remember about Granville?'

Jefferson had to concentrate for a few seconds to clear the fog in his brain.

'The last thing I remember? Um, I'm being held upside-down over a bathtub. Red is holding me by the ankles and Mackie's trapped me with his knee. Red has got a big knife in his hand and . . .'

At these words, he gave a faint groan, 'Aaaaagh!' His eyes filled with tears. He wasn't likely to forget that nightmare in a hurry. Gilbert placed a hand on his shoulder.

'Yeah, we arrived in the nick of time, that's for certain! You can thank Walter Schmitt and all the others for that.'

'Then I can vaguely picture myself lying in the bathtub with your faces leaning over me. After that, I don't recall anything . . .'

Gilbert made him laugh when he told him about the phenomenal storming of the apartment and the jerky coach drive home, with him, Gilbert, at the wheel. Their arrival in the middle of the night had been a sorry sight, but the following morning everything had gone crazy.

The two humans had been thoroughly interrogated by the canine police. After denying everything, and then accusing each other for half a day, they had finally confessed and the truth about the murder came out. It was indeed Mackie who'd killed Mr Edgar. His fingerprints on the scissors were proof. That morning, he'd made an appointment at the salon like a normal customer and had asked Mr Edgar to shave his beard. Mrs Kristiansen was already asleep under the dryer. She hadn't seen or heard anything. Red stood outside, keeping a lookout. Mackie had simply grabbed the scissors from a shelf and cold-bloodedly plunged them into Mr Edgar's chest. Because the hairdresser had collapsed without a sound, Mrs Kristiansen hadn't woken up. Luckily for her, in fact, because otherwise she'd have been skewered on the spot. Then, Mackie had bolted the door from the inside, to stop any customers from coming in and to delay the discovery of the body. Then he'd climbed out of the window at the back and fled at top speed with his accomplice.

'In short, I'm cleared?' concluded Jefferson.

'You're more than cleared! You're now the hero who was wrongly accused. By the way, Sophie asked if she can visit you. What do I tell her?'

'Um, I'd rather wait until I don't have this thing on my head any more. What is it, by the way? What's wrong with me?'

Gilbert burst out laughing.

'What's wrong with you? Let me tell you. Red's hand must have slipped when we stormed the apartment and he cut off your left ear. I picked it up and wrapped it in my handkerchief. A silky little triangle, the sweetest thing, you should have seen it! I was going to bring it with me to give to you as a souvenir . . . but Clarissa was much cleverer. She did the right thing. She put it in a Tupperware container filled with ice cubes, your cute little ear, and she gave it to them here, at the hospital. And they sewed it back on! So there you are!'

Over the next few days, there was a procession of visitors. First of all Jefferson's family members, led by his sister Chelsea, who was wearing the white skirt and sky-blue blouse he'd borrowed from her when he'd gone into town in disguise.

Then came a good number of the Globetrotters, in small groups of three or four. They hadn't lost touch with one another once they were home, as usually happens after most package tours. The high drama had created a bond between them. They were all saddened to see their little travel companion bundled up in his hospital bed. The bedside table was covered in their many gifts, which had to be piled up.

Requests for interviews were pouring in from journalists, but Jefferson only agreed to see one: the reporter who had insisted he was innocent and had written it in his newspaper. He was a young horse, with his tail plaited. Jefferson invited him to sit beside his bed and told him the whole story in detail, starting with the car that had almost crushed him right up to the capture of the two killers. Delighted, the horse scribbled madly, sometimes rubbing his aching wrist.

In the middle of their interview, Jefferson's phone vibrated on his bedside table. He apologised and reached out. The text message came from the humans' world, but he didn't recognise the sender's number. As for the message, it seemed to be in code:

Red squirrel with cap fled into forest . . . stop . . .
Hope animals arrived safely . . . stop . . . The struggle
goes on . . . stop . . . Here's to life . . .

One afternoon, Jefferson was snoozing in his hospital room when there was a knock on his door. Seeing Sophie come in, he was glad his enormous bandage had been removed that morning. Now he had only a light dressing over his sewn-on ear, held in place by a band around his forehead.

'Am I disturbing you?'

Oh, no, she wasn't disturbing him. Quite the

contrary. He sat up and leaned against his pillow and looked at her. Her eyes were still filled with sadness, he thought, but she looked lovely in her Cut 'n' Dye overalls, and her laryngitis was now just an unpleasant memory.

First of all, he told her where to find the postcard sent by Mr Edgar which was in his metal locker.

'I'm sorry, it's been handled a bit because I showed it to all the Globetrotters to convince them that I wasn't making things up. And I kept it on me all the time, like a lucky charm.

'And it seems to have worked?'

'Yes, it worked. We were very lucky!'

'You were very brave too. That's why I've come to see you. To tell you. And to thank you.'

Jefferson blushed with pride.

'Would you like a chocolate? I've been given loads. Help yourself.'

She took one and slowly unwrapped it.

'And also, I have some good news. In any case, I hope you'll think it's good news.'

'Tell me.'

She put the chocolate in her mouth and ate it thoughtfully.

'Well, my uncle had foreseen that something

might happen to him and so he drew up a will. I didn't know that. Guess what – he left me the salon. I hesitated for a few days and thought long and hard about it, but now I've decided: I'm taking over Cut 'n' Dye. As soon as the formalities are sorted out, bingo: it'll be re-opening!'

The cheerful *bingo* was accompanied by a wistful smile.

'You're doing the right thing!' exclaimed Jefferson. 'But don't be sad. Life must go on! Mr Edgar would have been delighted.'

'I know he would,' she said. 'I'd just like to change the name, to make a fresh start. I'm thinking of "Inspirations". I'll put a lovely portrait of my uncle in the salon.'

'I love the idea!' said Jefferson. 'And I'd love to be your first customer. I mean, I'd be a funny customer with my ear . . .'

She wiped her eyes. 'Oh, don't worry about that. You've got thick hair and it will be easy to conceal the scar, if there is one.'

They talked some more about Mr Edgar and his secret.

'I'd never have imagined that of him,' she confessed. 'But it doesn't surprise me. He was generous and philosophical. Campaigning to protect animals was just like him.'

Jefferson nodded but didn't dare say what was bothering him. During his long, idle hours in the hospital, he was haunted by images of the abattoir: those hundreds of thousands of animals slaughtered every day, those tormented sheep and battered pigs, those cows in the silence of the night, waiting to die. Taking over Mr Edgar's salon was very nice, for sure, but continuing his struggle would be even better. Only how to broach the subject?

'Oh yes,' he said after a silence, 'I brought you something back from there, but you'll have to go into my locker again.'

He directed her until she found her present. She unwrapped it. It was a glass ball containing a miniature district of Granville, the canal area, with the houses with coloured facades where Mr Edgar had rented a room. When you turned it upside down, snow fell silently onto the rooftops.

17

Jefferson found his cottage just as he'd left it two weeks earlier. As he unlocked the door, he had the feeling he'd been gone for months. So much had happened in such a short time.

He took off his shoes in the hall, placing first his right and then his left foot on the stool, put on his slippers, hung his jacket on the hook and went into the kitchen. In the oven, his potato dish had turned into a sad mush with a blackened crust. Yuck. He threw it into the bin. Then he sank down onto his sofa and stayed there for a moment, sitting perfectly still, feeling a little gloomy, to tell the truth. At times during the trip he'd missed his solitude. He had often pictured going home, the peace and quiet, free at last from the schedule and having to be at certain places at certain times, free to do nothing, without even

Gilbert at his side. But now he was back home, he missed the group, the bursts of chatter and laughter.

He was dwelling on these thoughts when his phone rang. Gilbert probably. No, it was Clarissa the hen.

'Hello, Jefferson. I heard you've left hospital and I wanted to invite you to a party next week.'

'A party? But . . . what sort of party?'

'Well, we've hired a hall, in town. When I say "we", I mean the Globetrotters, of course. It'll be an opportunity to meet up again and swap photos of Granville. Everyone will bring a dish and we'll have a sort of buffet . . . Do you like the idea? You can bring someone if you like.'

Of course he liked the idea! When he rang off, he realised that he was grinning from ear to ear. He already knew who he'd invite and what dish he'd bring.

He arrived at the hall on the day, carrying his potato dish covered in aluminium foil.

A little stage had been set up with a screen as a backdrop. The buffet table was groaning under the weight of all the starters, hot dishes and desserts. The two vixens were DJ-ing, playing music at full volume. Some tables were laid, and several Globetrotters were already seated at them. Jefferson did a quick tour of the room, greeting the Pearls, the Cousins, the Hilds and a few others, then sat down beside Simone. She'd saved him a place and left him no choice. 'My dear bodyguard,' she still called him fondly. She gave a little forced smile when Sophie came to sit with them.

Once everyone was there, Gilbert, beaming all over his face, grabbed the mic and launched into a reasonably coherent speech. He said he'd had the best and most exciting week of his life.

Then they projected the photos which Rupert the cat had put together in a skilful slide show. The first shot showed the dawn departure on the very first morning, when they didn't know one another yet. There was Roland, piling the suitcases into the Globetrotters' coach luggage compartment.

'I had no idea what I'd be putting in my luggage compartment on the way back!' he said.

Then there were some lovely shots of the countryside, and then of Granville, with its ancient streets, its canal, bridges and cathedral. But the photos they liked best by far were those showing the Globetrotters themselves!

They laughed heartily on seeing Mrs Cousins, her eyes popping out of her head in front of the breakfast buffet; Roland having a snooze behind the wheel, his peak pulled down over his eyes; the two vixens, heads down, engrossed in their phones during a cultural tour; the hosepipe that had caused Mrs Schmitt to fall off her bike in the park; Simone posing reluctantly in front of Simone's Haberdashery; Mr Hild caught surreptitiously throwing a misshapen macaron into the bin. There was applause for Roxanne, with her flaming hair, talking enthusiastically in front of the cathedral. They became emotional watching the Pearls crying as Clarissa presented them with their anniversary gift.

But all that was nothing in comparison to the dozen photos that Rupert had managed to take when they'd stormed the apartment. The first one showed Walter Schmitt rushing at the front door like a cannonball.

'That's when I did my shoulder in!' he exclaimed, laughing. 'That's when I did my shoulder in!'

They saw Clarissa, her arms raised outside the bathroom, shrieking, 'They're in here! They're in here!'; then came the two goats rushing headlong at Red; and there was Jefferson, his face covered in blood, in the arms of Doctor Cousins; they saw Roland hauling Mackie by his feet into the lift; Gilbert again, wild-eyed, gripping the steering wheel on leaving Granville.

The final shot was very dark. It showed Roland, standing on one leg at the police station gates, in the silence of the night, pressing the buzzer with his forefinger.

They turned the lights back on. There was a silence, during which they were probably all thinking the same thing: *Was that really us? Did we do that?* Yes, it was they who'd done that, all together.

Deeply moved, Jefferson discreetly blew his nose. He had no idea that the most dramatic part of the evening was still to come. Clarissa the hen clambered up onto the stage and seized the mic.

'Right, and now, dear Jefferson, I have – *we* have – a little surprise for you. Because most importantly, this is your party, isn't it? It's to celebrate your innocence. So, we tried something that your friend Gilbert whispered in our ear. Something impossible. But sometimes the impossible is possible, as we've all seen! So here, hold on to your seat! This is for you.'

They turned the lights off again and, this time, a film was projected onto the screen. The opening shot was of a forest, seen from a plane, a dense forest of a deep green, with a great river meandering lazily through it. The Amazonian forest, it seemed. Then the scene was deep inside the forest, walking through the vegetation. You could hear the unseen cameraman's breathing as he walked, and the swish of his machete, cutting a path. And finally, you saw him in profile, sitting cross-legged by a campfire on the riverbank in the evening. He was eating something that was hard to make out. He turned to the camera, smiling, to show it.

Chuck! It was Chuck!

Jefferson had read everything his hero had written, especially the thrilling *Alone on the River*, but he wasn't aware of any film. Seeing Chuck move and walk, hearing him speak and breathe, watching him set up camp, washing and giving a little wave before disappearing inside his mosquito net, in short, seeing him in action and so amazingly alive overwhelmed him. What a brilliant idea of Gilbert's! Nothing could have made him happier. Forgetting his shyness, he stood up and joined Clarissa on stage.

'Let me explain,' he said. 'I . . . well, I love reading and my favourite book is *Alone on the River*. The Orinoco is a river in South America, and that's what you've just seen. And I'm a huge admirer of this adventurer, yes, his name's Chuck and . . . yes, I didn't know about this film, it's . . . it's amazing.'

He turned to Clarissa.

'But how did you get hold of it? It's a private video, isn't it?'

'It is,' replied Clarissa. 'And we got hold of it because someone brought it here.'

'Someone?' asked Jefferson, and he felt a tingling in his hands.

'Yes, and this person, despite his tough character, is a bit like you, dear Jefferson: he is modest and shy. That's why he's been sitting at the back of the room since the start of the evening. But perhaps we could ask him to come forward now? What do you think?'

A tall, athletic-looking young man, a human, slowly walked the length of the room. He was wearing a simple pair of jeans and a black T-shirt. His fair hair tumbled over his shoulders. He leaped up onto the stage without using the steps, and within seconds was at Jefferson's side. He bent very low to give Clarissa a kiss, and then shook Jefferson's hand. The difference in size and build was spectacular.

Chuck – because that's who it was – took the mic from Clarissa's hand.

'Yes, it's footage I took on the Orinoco, but I have never shown it. It's private. And now I'm going to explain how I came to be here with you this evening. I must tell you, Jefferson, because you look a little . . . how can I say . . . a little surprised.'

That made everyone laugh, because Jefferson didn't look merely surprised. He looked dumbfounded, gobsmacked, astonished, blown-away, flabbergasted, staggered, amazed, shocked, dazed and confused. He'd thought Chuck was a fictional character so it was quite simply impossible for him to be there beside him in flesh and blood. It was a pure miracle.

'When Gilbert telephoned me,' continued Chuck, 'I nearly put the phone down immediately, but for some reason, I listened. He's very convincing, is Gilbert! He found the right words. First of all he told me that Jefferson had said *Alone on the River* was the best book he'd ever read. Is that true, Jefferson?'

Jefferson nodded.

'I was moved by that,' Chuck went on. 'So I let him tell me your whole story from the beginning. I found it – what's the word? – enthralling. I thought you were very courageous. It made me laugh too. In short, I said to myself: *I must do something* and I thought of sending you a signed copy of my book. And then Gilbert explained why Mr Edgar had been murdered, and that changed everything. He told me about his night at the abattoir. I knew all that. We talk about it in our world. Photos circulate online. But I'm afraid people cover their eyes and ears. In any case, I've been thinking about it these past few days and asking myself whether I should stop eating meat.'

Applause broke out, interrupting him for a moment.

'As for Mr Edgar, I fear he's irreplaceable, but I could use my modest fame to take up his fight and defend the cause, back home, in the world of the humans. I'm going to give it some serious thought, I promise you.' He paused. 'OK, I don't want to spoil your fun, and besides, you're not the ones who need to be troubled with all that, it's not your fault, after all.'

'You're not spoiling our fun,' broke in Clarissa. 'Quite the opposite, thanks to you, tonight will be unforgettable.'

'It will be for me too,' said Chuck. 'To think I've been to the Amazon eight times but I've never been here, to your land, just a seven-hour drive from Granville.'

'Fourteen when Gilbert's at the wheel!' shouted Walter Schmitt from the back of the room.

'There you are,' concluded Chuck. 'I'm delighted to be with you this evening and, through Jefferson, I embrace you all.'

So saying, he leaned over, grabbed Jefferson by the shoulders, raised him up to his height and kissed him on both cheeks. Then he clasped him to his chest long enough for the animals to clap and take photos.

Nestling against Chuck's chest, Jefferson could feel his heart beating in his own. It was crazy. All because one fine morning, he'd had the idea of going to get his quiff trimmed!

As he was leaving the hall, giddy with emotion, he ran into Sophie, who was also leaving. She said, 'Are you leaving, Jefferson? Because I was thinking, I mean, I was *wondering* whether perhaps . . . I mean . . . we could go for one last drink together . . .'